Lying Under the Stars
(and Spying on Mrs. Kirby)

Sharon Love Cook

Author: Sharon Love Cook
Cover photo: Ignatio Agiular
Electronic layout: Polgarus Studio

Published by Neptune Rising Press
900 Cummings Center, Suite #404-T
Beverly, Massachusetts 01915

ONE

Eight thirty at night and I was on my stomach in the tall beach grass watching the Kirby cottage. The sand was cold under me; the grass was wet. I was glad I'd worn jeans. If it'd been warmer, I'd have enjoyed being here, listening to the waves crashing on the beach and the tree toads chirping. April in New England can be pretty raw. At least it was a clear night, perfect for surveillance. Just when I thought about giving up and going home, Mrs. Kirby appeared at the kitchen window. For a moment I thought I'd have a heart attack, if that's possible at fourteen. She struggled with a big pot, emptying it into the sink. Steam fogged the window pane, making her look like a teenager and not the older woman she is, probably twenty-nine, or even thirty. She brushed her hair from her forehead, like she was exhausted.

No doubt her husband, who I call "El Stubbo," was complaining in the background: "Where's my dinner,

Nancy?" Meanwhile, her little kid, who I call "El Snotto," was making a racket, banging on his highchair. He was probably demanding: "Where's my dinner, Mommy?"

Poor Mrs. Kirby is too good for them. She deserves more than a cottage off-season with a whiny kid, a smelly old dog, and a husband who wears sweatshirts with the sleeves torn off.

Ouch! Something bit me. I hoped I wasn't lying on top of an ant hill. They built extensive tunnels under the sand. Yet, no matter what, I'd trained myself to be still. I was practicing to become a surveillance expert. Although I'd only been observing the Kirbys' cottage for three weeks, I'd amassed a lot of information.

For instance: husband Frank (El Stubbo), was a troubleshooter for a utility company. The kid, Ryan (El Snotto), went to The Fuzzy Caterpillar nursery school three days a week. Butchie, the family dog, was an old beagle mix with a nasty bark. Last but not least, the beautiful Mrs. Kirby (Nancy), studied psychology at the local community college.

Watching Mrs. Kirby, I was aware she was unhappy. When she was at the sink doing the dishes, the look on her face said it all. Meanwhile, El Stubbo sat nearby, watching TV and flossing his teeth. He had no idea his wife was miserable because Mrs. Kirby was a good sport. When he came up behind her and wrapped those gorilla arms around her, she smiled bravely. It was times like those when I wanted to save her.

The Red Army ants must have been on the move; something tickled my belly button. Next they'd be down my pants. It was getting late anyway. I didn't want Mom wondering where I was. As I was about to slink away through the grass, I spotted something on the clothesline near the back porch. Hanging among the dish towels, kids' socks, and El Stubbo's US Marines t-shirt was something black and silky swaying in the breeze. It called to me.

Now, the first rule of surveillance was: *Don't draw attention to yourself.* As a creature of the night, I was normally cautious. Professional. I didn't take risks because it was dumb. The black panties, however, had hijacked my brain.

I made a quick decision—go for it. Thus I pivoted, changing direction and moving toward the house. My belly skimmed the cool, wet grass. Eight seconds later, the blood pulsing in my head, I was pressed against the Kirbys' damp concrete foundation. It smelled of mildew. Two seconds later I was under the clothes line. My hand shot up like a cobra's tongue to snatch the prize. At the same time, a plastic clothespin bounced off my head.

With the soft, silky material crushed in my fist, I swiveled and headed toward the dune. Halfway there, a screen door slammed. The night's silence was shattered by loud, staccato barking. *Butchie!* My mouth went dry as I watched him making a beeline for me, yapping shrilly.

"Quiet!" I hissed when he got near. He didn't stop. Instead, he circled me, growling. Finally he clamped his graying muzzle onto the leg of my jeans. He growled and attacked the material, tugging and shaking his head back and forth. I kicked out and he growled louder, tightening his vice-like grip. In desperation, I threw sand in his face. He responded by pulling harder.

The overhead light on the front porch went on. The screen door creaked. Mrs. Kirby, sounding worried, called, "Butchie!"

The sweat in my armpits froze. I grabbed the dog's collar with one hand, praying he wouldn't bite. With the other, I slipped the panties over his head, covering his face. The elastic material clung to his muzzle. When I released him he yelped, dropping his hold on my jeans. He backed away, shaking his head.

With that, I slithered to the grassy embankment atop the dune. Before going over, I looked back. Mrs. Kirby held the screen door open. Butchie, the panties on his head, trotted up the steps. I caught the look of surprise on her face, but I didn't hang around.

One second later I was cascading down the dune like a log over a waterfall. At the bottom, I leaped to my feet. Ahead was a neighboring cottage, dark and shuttered. I raced for the shadows under the porch and stood there, my heart pounding from the close call.

When heavy clouds moved in front of the moon, providing temporary cover, I sprinted for the boardwalk. There I ran along the concrete walkway, passing dark, boarded-up cottages. The ocean, on my right, was black with tiny lights bobbing far out on the horizon. At the end of the boardwalk, I skipped down the dozen steps to the bottom. I sat on a cool, concrete step, resting until I caught my breath.

My bike was hidden behind the old boat shack adjacent to the salt marsh. I pulled it out. The seat was slick with dew. I performed a quick check, making sure no slugs were clinging to the underside. One night, while riding home, I'd glanced down to see a slimy slug inching up my thigh. I almost went over the handlebars.

I set out. Halfway down the road, the moon appeared from behind the clouds. It lit up the trees and rooftops with a silver glow. In the distance, the waves crashed on the beach, making a hissing sound when they retreated.

I continued along the dirt road until I was behind the Kirbys' cottage. There I stopped. Mrs. Kirby was silhouetted against the kitchen window shade. I closed my eyes and sent her a message: *Don't worry. I'll save you.*

TWO

When I reached my house, I saw Doreen's Honda Civic, with its bumper sticker reading "*Get Offa My Ass!*" parked in the driveway. Doreen is my mom's best friend from high school. Although they graduated in 1975, twenty-four years ago, they act like they're still back in school.

I entered the darkened kitchen through the side door. Down the hall, in the den, the music of Neil Diamond blasted from the stereo. I tiptoed to the door and peeked inside. Mom and Doreen, wearing velour jogging suits, were sprawled on the furniture, their eyes closed. Each held a wine glass. The smoke hanging in the air made them look like ghostly figures. I didn't know which was worse, the smoke or the music.

Doreen spotted me first. "Jeez, Christopher, you wanna give me a heart attack?" She grabbed her wine glass before it ended up on the shag rug.

Mom, squinting through the haze, leaped to her

feet. "Chris is home. Butts out, Doreen." She went to the window and raised it high.

"I put mine out long ago," Doreen said. "I'm not a chain smoker like *some* people."

"If you had my problems, you would be." Mom fanned the night air into the room. "Where have you been, Christopher? I've been worried sick."

Doreen saved me from answering by saying, "Get used to it, Ginger. The boy's in high school now. It's normal for kids to pull away, become independent."

Mom ignored this bit of advice and turned to me. "Well?"

"I was at Evan's." The lie came naturally.

"You're telling me *Mrs. Murray* let you stay this late?"

"We were outside," I explained, "setting up bike jumps."

They both stared at me. I felt like a bug in a jar. "I'm sorry. We were having fun. I lost track of time."

Doreen spoke up. "Christopher's a good kid. He's not like we used to be, wild and wacky. Remember, Ginger, how my dad called us—"

"Didn't you say you had to get up early?" Mom stared at the clock on the wall.

Doreen laughed and stretched her arms over her head. Her shirt rode up over a belly that looked like melted mozzarella. "Okay, I can take a hint. Just remember that kids today want honesty from their parents." She put an arm around me. "Isn't that right, honey?"

What I wanted was invisibility from my parents, 'though I said, "I guess."

"You betcha." She squeezed me hard. I tried not to yelp.

After Doreen left, I helped Mom clean up the den. As always, she complained about Doreen. "She's got her nerve, telling me how to raise my own son. Why is it that childless people think they're experts on parenting?"

I didn't respond, nor did she expect an answer. Instead, I carried glasses, plates, and ashtrays to the kitchen. Everything got shoved into the dishwasher. Then, I said good night and headed upstairs.

I got into my pajamas and went into the bathroom. After brushing my teeth, I put anti-zit lotion on a cotton ball and rubbed it over my face and neck. Back in my room, I dragged a trunk out from under the bed. The top section held a stack of *Fangoria* magazines. I reached for a hidden section under that, where I hid my surveillance notebook.

On a new line I recorded the date and a brief description of what had happened tonight at Granite Cove Beach. I was disappointed I'd given in to my impulse of capturing the black panties. On the other hand, it'd been worth it. At the same time I felt a pang, losing them to Butchie. Had I won them, I'd have put them under my pillow.

I forced myself to think about something else. From my reading of *Beginner's Buddhism*, I've learned it's pointless to dwell on losses. All misery arises from attachment. Although I'd only held the panties for a minute, I'd grown attached.

I got into bed thinking about Mrs. Kirby. I imagined her at the kitchen sink, wearing a bikini, her lipstick the color of red licorice. She was alone and facing a huge pile of (El Stubbo's) dirty dishes. I happened to be walking near her cottage, my fishing pole over my shoulder. (Striper fishermen often go out at night, casting their lines from the shore.)

As Mrs. Kirby struggled with a big, scummy lobster pot, it slipped from her wet hands and hit the floor. From the seawall, I heard the crash and Mrs. Kirby cry out. I dropped my pole and rushed to her door, calling, "Mrs. Kirby, is everything all right?"

With tears running down her face, she opened the door. "Oh, Christopher, no one can help me." To my amazement, she rushed into my arms, warm and soapy—

My daydream was interrupted by a voice outside: "Christopher, are you awake?"

I groaned. It was Mom, calling me. I dragged myself from bed and sank to my knees at the window. She stood underneath, leaning against the vinyl siding and smoking. I looked down. "Hi, Mom."

"Honey, is the smoke drifting into your room?"

"No," I lied.

She was quiet for a moment. Then she said, "Christopher, are you happy here?"

"Yeah."

"Seriously, is this where you really want to live, here with me?"

"Uh-huh."

"You don't ever think about living with your father?"

"Nope." I yawned. "I'm going to sleep now, Mom."

"Okay, sweetheart. Love you. Good night."

"Yup. Night."

I got back into bed. Something was up.

My mom has trouble getting up mornings. On TV sitcoms, it's always the mother who drags the kid out of bed. At our house, it's my job. "Move your butt!" is my final call before rushing out the door to catch the school bus. With no one around to force her, Mom finally gets up. She's lucky her boss is a geezer who doesn't arrive early at the office.

After boarding the bus, I scanned the seats, looking for Evan. When I didn't see him, I sat in the first row, behind the bus driver. She's got four framed magnetic photos stuck to the dashboard. They're pictures of the fattest baby I've ever seen. His legs have folds like a Sumo wrestler's. His baby outfits are probably size XXXXL.

Shawna Curran, who sucks up to teachers and everyone, asked the driver what's his name. "Sebastian," the bus driver said. "We call him 'Sebbie.'"

"That's so *cute*," Shawna squealed in her phony voice.

Now I leaned my head against the bus window. My forehead bounced off the pane with every bump in the road. Despite that, I dozed.

My first class was Computer Arts. I slid into the seat next to Evan. "Where were you this morning?" I whispered.

"My mom drove me," he said.

Maybe I was paranoid, but I thought Mrs. Murray drove Evan so he wouldn't associate with me. Ever since my parents' divorce, she wouldn't let Evan come to my house. "No supervision," was her excuse. Well, duh; that was why it was so fun.

Sitting at the desk in front of us was Vinnie Madruga, the class greaser. He was rarely in school, but when he was, he made sure everyone knew it. Now he turned and said, "Dude, check it out." He leaned back in his chair so we could see his computer monitor. On the screen was a lady in a gold thong and little else doing gymnastics. We stared at the image. Automatically I glanced at Mr. Fontaine, our teacher, on the other side of the room. He had on the same corduroy sports jacket, shiny from wear. Under that, a gray turtleneck. Even his hair was lame. It looked like a bird's nest fallen from a tree that settled on his head.

Vinnie motioned to the guys seated behind us. They dutifully got up. Basically, they were afraid of Vinnie, who was older than us. Someone claimed he was seventeen—and still a freshman.

Before long a group had gathered around his chair, laughing and nudging him. Vinnie acted like he'd created the image. In fact, he'd gotten it off a disk sneaked into class. Mr. Fontaine warns us not to bring in outside disks. They could contaminate the school's computers. Vinnie, who lives to break the rules, doesn't care. His goal was to create a disturbance, one requiring Mr. Fontaine's intervention. Vinnie not only bullied students, but those teachers who feared him.

Now Mr. Fontaine, unable to avoid the commotion going on, turned. He frowned. ""Mr. Madruga, have you located a graphic for your newspaper article?""

Vinnie paused, making sure he had the room's attention. "Yeah, I was just showing it to my classmates." The guys around him laughed.

"You boys take your seats," Mr. Fontaine said, his face flushed. As he neared Vinnie's desk, he spotted the lady in the thong. Sweat beads popped out on his forehead. "If Ms. Carbone sees that, she'll report you for sexual harassment."

"Yeah? Well, this ain't Ms. Carbone." Vinnie looked back at his buddies but they were settling in their seats.

Mr. Fontaine clapped his hands. "All right, young people, you've had your fun. Now get to work. No one leaves until I've signed off on your project."

Students groaned at his warning, and the room

grew quiet. No one wanted to stay behind. The class settled down to complete the assignment.

Vinnie, having lost the spotlight, got up and stood at the printer. He collected the copies he'd made of the thong lady. He looked around. When he realized no one was watching, he stuffed them into his back pocket. Then he headed for the exit, whistling. At the door, he said, "See ya, losers," and walked out. The tension in the room subsided.

I whispered to Evan, "How come Vinnie can do that, walk out of class without getting in trouble?"

"Because Fontaine's scared to report him," Evan whispered back. "He sits down to pee."

My last class of the day, English, was my favorite, for two reasons: I liked writing and I liked Mr. Ryan, our teacher. He was the coolest guy. He was young, compared to the other faculty fossils. His hair was long, though not too long. It was like he needed a trim but was too busy to get one. Mr. Ryan always wore a jacket and tie in class, unlike Sweatpants Spiddle, the history and gym teacher.

Mr. Ryan's teaching style was old-school. After we got the boring stuff—grammar and punctuation—out of the way, he had us write about a different topic every week. We started the essay in class and finished at home. I always did my English homework first. Sometimes I thought about the assignment while working at Save 'n' Rave.

I wasn't the only student who liked Mr. Ryan. Shawna Curran, who sat across from me, was a goody-girl in his classroom. "Can I talk to you, Mr. Ryan?" she asked, flipping her long, blond hair over her shoulder like a supermodel. Meanwhile, she was completely different in Mr. Fontaine's class. There she made farting noises. Not many girls could do that, especially pretty girls like Shawna.

Ms. Carbone, the bimbo of the business department, also thought Mr. Ryan was great. She strutted into his classroom every chance she got. Last week she asked, "Mr. Ryan, could you check the thermostat in my room? It doesn't seem to be working."

After he followed her out, Vinnie stood up. He stuck out his chest and wiggled his butt, imitating Ms. Carbone. He said, "Ooh, Mr. Ryan, it's so hot in my room. I've gotta cool off." Then he unbuttoned his shirt and swiveled his hips while humming stripper music. Although Vinny was a show-off and a bully, it was pretty funny.

Although I'd never have admitted it to anyone, not even to best-friend Evan, I thought Mr. Ryan was good-looking. I wasn't attracted to him or anything like that (I would never have spied outside his house). I just wished I could be like him when I grew up.

After we talked about composition, Mr. Ryan gave us our essay assignment: write about a disappointing event in our lives. I had plenty of those. However, what I really wanted to write about was Mrs. Kirby. Obviously, I'd have to make it up. Mr. Ryan didn't say it had to be true. I'd write about Nancy, my former girlfriend who got sick and died. I picked up my pen, imagining our last night together.

It was a hot August night. Nancy was weak, yet she wanted one last dance with me. I turned on the stereo. We danced in her living room, a slow song by Neil Diamond. Her parents, meanwhile, were sleeping upstairs.

The ceiling fan whirled above us. Strands of her silky hair stuck to my sweaty face. I didn't mind. I held her in my arms, supporting her. We danced so slowly we were practically standing still. When the song ended, the room got quiet. All we could hear were the crickets chirping outside and her parents snoring upstairs.

Nancy leaned against me. "Let's rest a moment." I guided her to the sofa. She kicked off her shoes and stretched out, her eyes gazing into mine as she reached for me. "Hold me, Christopher, just once, before I leave you for good..."

I crumpled the paper up, stuffing it into my pocket. Mr. Ryan would think I was a weirdo, taking advantage of a sick girl. Not only that, he'd know it wasn't true. The man's got a great BS detector.

What I would have liked to write about was my recent disappointment: losing the black silk panties to a dog. But how could I explain being outside Mrs. Kirby's cottage and stealing from her clothes line? Although Mr. Ryan wouldn't judge me, he'd think I was a strange kid.

You're only as sick as the secrets you keep. I read that message on an herbal teabag. If it was true, then I must be pretty sick.

THREE

Three afternoons a week, I worked at Save 'n' Rave market. It was an old store with linoleum floors and fluorescent lights that made the customers look embalmed. Or maybe they looked that way because they were old, most of them. They lived downtown, riding to the store in scooters and wheelchairs.

Mr. Zagrobski, the store manager, told us to keep an eye on certain shoppers who were known to steal. One day, as I knelt stocking cans, I saw an old guy stuff a salmon steak down his pants. He wore "grandpa" jeans with an elastic waist. I was supposed to find Mr. Zagrobski and report what I'd seen. What would Mr. Zagrobski do, make the guy drop his pants? In the end, I did nothing.

Although I complain about my job, it was where I first saw Mrs. Kirby. Now I kept breath mints in my pocket for when she appeared, which wasn't often. I get confused and sweaty when I see her. I don't trust myself to speak.

Wednesday after work, I was unlocking my bike from the rack when Mom drove up in her SUV. She rolled down the window, telling me she'd take me home. She held a wad of tissues clamped to her nose. Uh-oh, it had to be big for Mom to show up at work. On the other hand, my mom's the world's biggest drama queen.

In the end, I loaded my bike into the back of her car. I wasn't looking forward to the ride home. My stomach felt like it was digesting rocks.

We drove for a while, Mom sniffing but saying nothing. I knew she'd eventually tell me. As we left the downtown area, she pulled over to the curb and shifted into park. Resting her forehead on the steering wheel, she cried, "Oh Chris, you have no idea how miserable I am."

"What's wrong?" I reached over and shut off the ignition.

"It's your father."

I figured. It was always about Dad when she was miserable. "What's he done?"

She blew her nose. Bits of wet tissue sprayed the dashboard. "He's gotten a high-profile lawyer and he's filing for custody."

"You mean ... custody of me?" Duh, who else? I was their only child.

She nodded. "I was talking to Mr. Farley about it this afternoon. He said fathers today have a good chance in court."

"Mom, don't worry. I'll tell the judge I don't want to live with my dad, that I'm happy where I am."

"I wish it were that easy. Mr. Farley said the court considers lots of things, especially the child's environment."

"So, what's wrong with my environment?"

She paused to wipe her eyes. "Apparently, my smoking is a big factor."

I shrugged. "So you quit. You're always saying you want to quit anyway."

That wasn't the right thing to say. Mom started crying again. Finally, she said, "How can I quit smoking with a custody battle going on? I don't even have a lawyer."

"What about Mr. Farley? He's a lawyer." Mom had worked for Mr. Farley since she was in high school, typing deeds and stuff like that.

"Mr. Farley's a real estate lawyer. What does he know about custody? Not only that, he's eighty years old, for God's sake."

"He probably won't charge much," I said, trying to be positive.

She sighed. "He won't charge anything. How can he? I barely get by on a secretary's salary, plus child support." She looked at me, her face as long as a Basset hound's. "It's not fair."

I thought about what she'd told me, my mind spinning like a gerbil in a cage. I wished I'd never accepted her offer of a ride. I wished I was back at work, stocking shelves. Finally, I said, "It's okay, Mom. Mr. Farley will help us."

I didn't have much faith in that statement. Things didn't look good. My dad had been critical of Mom since he moved out. He called her a bad "role model" and a scatterbrain. Mom, in turn, called him a nerd. "Look up the word in the dictionary," she says. "You'll see a picture of your father."

She had a point. Ever since Dad moved in with my grandparents, he'd been acting like them. For instance, when we went out to lunch. He asked for a doggy bag even though it was a half-slice of pizza. He grabbed extra sugar packets and napkins, stuffing them in his pockets. And though Dad claimed he was caring for his parents, I thought it was the other way around. My grandmother treated him like a child. She even ironed his boxer shorts.

Thinking about all that, I asked Mom, "What if Dad won custody? Where would I live?"

"With his parents, of course. He wouldn't leave them now."

Her words made me shiver. Live in that dark house in the woods, with creaky stairs, old-people smells, and *no cable*? What was worse, I wouldn't see Mrs. Kirby. Granite Cove Beach was too far to bike from their house.

I felt panicky, yet forced myself to be calm. For better or worse, Mom and I were a team. One of us had to keep a cool head. I said, "I'll talk to Dad tomorrow when he picks me up for dinner. If it's the two of us, he'll listen."

Her mind was elsewhere. "You know what? I think your father is planning to use his secret weapon in court."

"What secret weapon?"

"I'm talking about Sherrie."

"His girlfriend? What about her?"

"I think they're going to get married. It would give him a stronger case. In court, Sherrie would make an impressive witness. Courts like teachers."

I snickered. Sherrie might fool a judge. She'd even fooled my grandparents. They thought she was an angel because she knitted ugly vests for Gramps. She also helped him exercise his dead arm (that he got following a stroke). If Dad won custody, I'd have to help exercise that arm.

I promised myself it wouldn't happen. For emphasis, I pounded the dashboard. "Don't worry, Mom. We'll beat this thing together."

She gave me a shaky smile. "We will?"

"Yup. Don't worry about it."

Mom reached over and ruffled my hair. She smiled and started the car. I must have sounded awfully convincing.

Every Thursday since he moved out, Dad had picked me up and taken me to my grandparents' house for dinner. Each night seemed to go on forever. At the end of the evening, I felt old. When I looked in the mirror, I was surprised to see a fourteen-year-old kid looking back, and not an eighty-year-old man with hair sticking out of his ears.

My dad didn't mind living at my grandparents' house. Maybe he was too busy to notice that their toilet seat was so old it belonged in a museum. And what about the creepy animal heads on the walls of the living room? And how about all the dim light bulbs? They made the place look like the setting of a horror movie. Perhaps my father had gotten as clueless as Gramma and Gramps.

Mom claimed the divorce was just an excuse for Dad to move back to his childhood home. Now he slept in his old bed surrounded by his high school sports trophies. Dad, on the other hand, claimed that Mom lives in the past. She was stuck in high school, where she was popular and voted "Best Dancer" and "Most Friendly." He said Mom's interests revolved around Saturday night: dancing and partying.

After listening to them fighting all the time, I was relieved when Dad moved out. Yet I also hoped they'd get back together, especially at Christmas. I pictured Dad arriving on our doorstep Christmas Eve, his arms full of presents, his hair covered with snow. I'd jump into his arms and we'd share a group hug like the family in *It's a Wonderful Life*.

To be fair, it wasn't too terrible at my grandparents' house. I liked the attention I got. Gramma fetched everything for me. She watched me and asked, "More gravy, Christopher? More butter for your mashed potatoes?"

My grandparents were from Finland. I didn't know if it was a Scandinavian tradition, but their food was pale: creamed corn, mashed potatoes, tuna noodle casserole, cucumbers in sour cream, tapioca pudding with whipped cream, among other dishes.

When Sherrie, Dad's girlfriend, was with us, she'd cut up Gramps' food. Like I mentioned, his arm was paralyzed from a stroke. When it happened, Dad was at Wentworth College studying engineering. He had to drop out to help run the family hardware store. Otherwise, Gramps could have injured himself and not even known it.

Once I asked my dad, "What would happen if Gramps put his hand on a red-hot oven. Wouldn't he feel it?"

Dad said he wouldn't feel it; he'd smell his skin burning. After that, I couldn't stop thinking about the dead arm. I'm glad Gramps keeps it in a sling, out of sight.

Now, Gramps said, "Ma, give Christopher a piece of banana cream pie. He's too skinny." He reached over and pinched my ribs. I yelped, yet resisted the urge to pinch his bony nose. Instead, I took a slow breath and held it for a count of five before letting it out. I learned that on the TV yoga show. The instructor wore a peach-colored body suit that looked like skin.

The slow breathing calmed me. I vowed to not let my grandfather's teasing get to me. He couldn't help being old and simple-minded. Dad says it was his way of having fun with me. I didn't mind, up to a point. What I minded were the subtle comments about my mom.

Tonight was no different. When Gramma set a massive slice of pie in front of me, Gramps said, "If you lived with us, you'd have banana cream pie every night."

"Thanks," I said. "If you didn't live so far from my school, maybe I would."

Gramps mulled this over. He couldn't drive because of his arm. Gramma never got her driver's license (although according to my mom, she tried *three times*).

Sherrie got up and carried dirty dishes into the kitchen. There she ran water into a basin. My grandparents, needless to say, don't have a dishwasher. Dad took a second helping of Swedish meatballs and noodles. The only sounds at the table were people chewing.

Gramma, referring to my earlier remark, said, "Your father could drop you off at school before opening the store."

That was ridiculous. Dad opened the store before seven, every morning except Sunday. When I reminded her of this fact, Gramps piped up: "Don't tell me *your mother* drives you to school every morning."

"Victor," Gramma said, hiding a smile.

"I get the bus," I told them once again. Every week at dinner, we end up having the same conversation. I jumped to my feet, saying, "I'm finished. Can I please watch TV now?"

Sherrie returned to the table, a dishtowel draped around her neck like a prize fighter. "You go in and relax, Chris."

I was about to thank her, but held my tongue. Sherrie didn't live there, yet she acted like it was her house. I headed for the TV room, crowded with dark heavy furniture. On a coffee table was a bowl of dusty Canada Mints that no one ever touched. I sank onto the sagging velvet sofa. It was the first time I'd been alone all day. I welcomed the solitude, although it didn't last long. Minutes later everyone else wandered in, discussing where to sit.

"What's on tonight, son?" Dad asked, collapsing next to me. Sherrie nudged him to move over. That left me squashed at the end, the wooden armrest digging into my side. Gramma took the chair opposite us. She fell asleep the second she sat down.

"I can't believe you guys don't have cable," I grumbled for the hundredth time. Not only that, the TV was an ancient model, the kind you see at yard sales. Wads of aluminum foil clung to the spiky antennae, supposedly for better reception.

Koski Hardware was a successful business. Why couldn't they break down and buy a new TV?

My dad squeezed my knee. "If you lived here, we'd get cable." He added, "You can have the room I slept in when I was your age."

Sherrie clapped her hands like a contestant on a game show. "Christopher, you lucky duck. I love that room."

My grandmother, her eyes closed, said, "We'd have to get a new mattress for that bed."

Gramps heaved his sling arm onto the armrest of his chair. "Nothing wrong with that mattress," he said.

"Nothing except it's over thirty-five years old," Gramma said.

"That's not old," he said. "My mother had a horsehair mattress for fifty-five years. When she died, it was still good—"

Gramma pointed at him. "He wanted to bring it into our home when we got married." She rolled her eyes. "That old thing had bugs!"

They continued fighting over the age and state of the mattress. I could see there would be no TV for me. I jumped up as if I'd sat on a hot spike and blurted out, "Listen, everyone, I'm happy where I'm living. I don't want to talk about it anymore."

They stopped and stared, surprised at my outburst. Gramma's eyes bulged like a stuffed haddock's. She opened her mouth but nothing came out. I ran from the room and up the stairs. At the top, I leaned over and took deep breaths. As I inhaled, their voices carried up to me. Sherrie was trying to calm everyone down.

I, too, had been shocked by my reaction. What had come over me? Was it the crowded room, everyone planning my future? Or had I gotten a glimpse of my future in that very room? Whatever it was, I'd freaked.

I went into the bathroom. At the sink I splashed cold water on my face. I rubbed my skin with a rough towel. Then I sat on the edge of the tub, feet propped on the toilet seat. It had to be an antique, the wood worn smooth with age. Although I understood my grandparents' unwillingness to splurge on a new TV, why couldn't they buy a new toilet seat? Koski Hardware sold toilet seats, for God's sake. Why hang onto a relic?

After a while, I decided to return downstairs to prove I wasn't having a meltdown. Passing the phone in the hall, I was tempted to call Mrs. Kirby, just to hear her voice. I could pretend I had a wrong number. Yet there was a chance she had caller ID, or she'd recognize my voice. I still remembered the first time she spoke to me. I was kneeling on the floor pasting labels on cans of Comet when I looked up. An angel hovered over me. The first thing I noticed was her perfume. It smelled like a meadow in springtime. It was nothing like my mom's perfume, so strong it would give a dog seizures.

I figured Mrs. Kirby was old because of a silver

streak in her dark hair. But her eyes were the blue of a swimming pool. When she looked at me, it was like I was drowning in them. Finally, the angel spoke: "Honey, do you sell twenty-five-pound bags of senior dog food?"

As I got to my feet, Mrs. Kirby held out her hand. Her skin was soft and silky. Together we walked to the pet food aisle, holding hands. She pointed out the brand of dog food she wanted. I said I'd check in the stock room out back. Reluctantly, I dropped her hand.

Inside the storage area, I wandered in a daze until finally I located the senior dog food. I offered to carry it to her car. After she checked out at the register, we headed for the parking lot, side by side. Mrs. Kirby talked about her dog, an old beagle mix with "digestive issues."

Her car, a dark blue wagon, had three stickers on the back window. One was a US Marines sticker; one was a parking sticker for Essex Community College; one was a Granite Cove Beach resident's sticker. When I opened the back and set the dog food inside, I spotted a kiddie seat. In Sherlock Holmes fashion, I deduced that the woman of my dreams had a husband, a kid, and a dog. My chances with her were slim to none, and slim just left town. In the event of a global nuclear disaster, with Mrs. Kirby and me the only humans left on the planet, she *still* wouldn't go out with me.

After setting the dog food down, I slammed the door. "What's your name?" she asked.

"Christopher Koski." I smiled, hoping my gums weren't showing. I hate when my gums show in school photos.

"I'm Nancy Kirby. Thank you very much, Christopher."

She held out a couple of bills. I instinctively reached for them. At the last minute I yanked my hand back. "No, thanks, Mrs. Kirby. I'm happy to help." The money drifted to the ground and I crouched to pick it up. When I stood, I stepped on my apron tie, resulting in a loud rip.

"Oh, dear. You've torn something," she said.

"No problem." I dangled the tie in case she thought it was my pants that had ripped.

"Let me sew that for you. It's the least I can do."

"That's okay. My mom will sew it." I quickly added, "Or my girlfriend."

She patted my shoulder before sliding into the driver's seat. As I watched her drive away, I mulled over my lost opportunity. Why hadn't I accepted her offer to sew my apron? It would have given me an excuse for further contact. Maybe I'd even visit her. I watched her car's taillights vanish and imagined my visit to Granite Cove Beach:

It was a beautiful spring day when Mrs. Kirby suggested a walk by the shore. We were alone, April being too early for residents or beach-goers. We walked to the end of the beach. There we sat on huge, sun-baked boulders, a soft ocean breeze blowing our hair.

Mrs. Kirby reached into a picnic basket she carried. "Surprise," she said, taking out a bottle of wine and two cheese-steak subs with onions and peppers. She handed me a glass. Pouring from the bottle, she said, "I hope you like French wine, Christopher."

"Is there any other kind?" I replied, raising an eyebrow like James Bond.

After we finished the cheese-steak subs, Mrs. Kirby took the empty wine glass from me. Looking into my eyes, she said, "No more wine, darling. More kisses."

She leaned toward me. Our lips touched ...

My daydream was ruined when Mr. Zagrobski came up behind me. "Chrissake, Koski, there you are. Whatsa matter? You in a coma?"

I sighed and followed him inside.

Now I went down my grandparents' stairs, careful to avoid any creaking. I tiptoed past the TV room and into the kitchen. There I stuck my finger into the remains of the banana cream pie and slowly licked off the cream. Finally, I couldn't delay my return to the TV room and the apology everyone was expecting.

As it turned out, I didn't need to apologize. When

I finally entered the room, everyone was asleep and snoring. The TV screen buzzed with static, as if a blizzard raged inside.

FOUR

In Computer Arts class, Mr. Fontaine handed out permission forms for the student reading in Boston. Mr. Fontaine would be one of the chaperones. Evan nudged me and asked, "Koski, you going?"

I hadn't given it a thought until I learned that Mr. Ryan was organizing the event. He selects the best two or three student essays from his classes. Ever since I learned about the reading, I've been thinking of nothing else. If Mr. Ryan chose my essay, it would be life-changing. Kids seeing me pass in the hall would say, "There's Christopher Koski, the prize-winning essay writer."

I told Evan I'd go, even if I had to ask my dad for the money.

"Cool," he said. "Let's sit together on the bus. Otherwise, we could end up next to Stefan, the exchange student."

"What's wrong with Stefan?"

"He doesn't wash his hair. He's got moths crawling around in there."

"Moths? I don't believe it."

"It's true. He lives with Todd Broadfoot's family. One morning, Mrs. Broadfoot found moths on Stefan's pillow."

"Maybe in his country they don't wash their hair," I said. "What did the Broadfoots do?"

"Mrs. Broadfoot bought some anti-bug shampoo. She wore rubber gloves when she used it on Stefan's head."

"That's wicked gross."

After discussing Stefan's moths, I was tempted to tell Evan about the custody suit. Although he would have understood, he would have felt sorry for me. Evan had been my best friend since second grade, but things had changed between us. It had started with his mother deciding our friendship was no longer wholesome, following my parents' divorce.

Mrs. Murray was like one of those phony TV moms. She drove Evan and his sister, Katrina, to school in the family minivan. She didn't want them exposed to the "bad element" that rode the bus. When Evan asked if he could go home with me, she made up excuses as to why he couldn't. My mom might be lame, but Evan's mom was evil. According to Mrs. Murray, the world was divided into two categories: things that were appropriate and things that were inappropriate. Following my parents' divorce, I joined the latter category.

While we looked over the class trip form, I

whispered to Evan, "You know who else is going as a chaperone?"

"Who?"

"Sno-Cones Carbone."

"Dude, maybe we can peek in the ladies' room window, take a picture of her *au naturel*." Evan liked to show off his French.

"If Ms. Carbone catches us," I said, "she'll beat us with her high-heeled shoe till our butt cheeks look like Swiss cheese."

"It'd be worth it," he said, elbowing me.

"It'd feel like this," I said, grabbing a pencil and poking him with the sharp end. He let out a shriek.

Mr. Fontaine, bent over a student's monitor, called out, "No more horseplay, young people, or you'll go to Mr. Dunbar's office."

We mumbled an apology. Mr. Dunbar, the principal, was a hard-ass. The only person not afraid of him was Vinnie Madruga.

We worked on our assignment. Evan, as always, was first to finish. He nudged me and whispered, "Maybe the ladies' room will be on the first floor. You can stand on my shoulders and look in the window."

I shook my head. "Mr. Ryan would lose faith in me."

At the mention of Evan's least-favorite teacher, he wrinkled his nose. "Do you think Ryan's got a thing for Ms. Carbone?"

"Are you kidding? He's going to be a famous

writer some day. She's keeping him from reaching his goals."

Evan chuckled. "Koz, sometimes you're so naive."

After class ended, we walked out together. I was about to head for the main exit when he said, "Hey, you working tomorrow after school?"

"Why, is Mommy letting you off the leash?"

He punched my arm. "Cut it out, butt-wipe. As a matter of fact, she's going to the Flower Show in Boston."

"Okay, you can come over."

"Maybe we could play Phone Freaks," he said.

"Cool," I said, concealing my excitement. Not only was Evan coming to my house after weeks of staying away, we'd play Phone Freaks, the best prank game in the world. What we did was pick out a really weird name from the phone book. For instance, we once found someone named "Hiram Wockenfuss," believe it or not. We'd learned that a dorky name was usually connected to a dorky person.

We called the person, pretending to be adults representing various companies. Because Evan was good at sounding old, he made the calls. Sometimes we said we were the electric company, notifying our victim that we were shutting off the power. Once we were Hollywood scouts with a movie company, searching locations. We said we wanted to use the person's house while filming a major motion picture. Before hanging up, we gave the homeowner a contact name, spelling it out. When she said the name out loud—"Ben Dover"—she swore and hung up.

Another good prank involved telling people we were from radio station WONK. They'd win a hundred dollars if they could sing the opening lines to a popular song. When they started singing, we almost peed our pants laughing.

Playing Phone Freaks was the most fun you could have at home. Evan and I were the perfect team to play it.

English was my last class of the day and my favorite. Making up stories about characters I'd created was so much fun I would have done it voluntarily. I had Mr. Ryan to thank. He made the subject interesting. Some kids thought he was a sorehead because he didn't joke around or try to be our buddy. Mr. Ryan was cool without even trying.

While we worked on our assignment, he sat at his desk, writing on a long, yellow, lined pad. I wished I knew what he was writing. Shawna Curran claimed he was working on a screenplay, but how did she know?

Before the end of class, he wrote some instructions on the board and said, "Copy this, because it concerns your final project."

Richie Digou, who sat in front of me, moaned out loud. He was the laziest kid, always moaning and groaning upon the mention of an assignment. I tried copying Mr. Ryan's instructions, but Richie's back was so broad I had to lean to one side to see around him.

Shawna, sitting next to me, whispered, "He is *so* gorgeous."

"You mean Richie?" I whispered back.

She smacked my arm with her fist. It hurt; Shawna plays lacrosse. "No, dummy," she hissed. "You know who I mean." With that, she flipped open her notebook. She'd covered a full page with frilly hearts. Inside were the words "Shawna & Rob forever."

"Rob," I whispered. "Is that Mr. Ryan's name?"

She nodded. "It's short for Robert. Anything else you'd care to know?"

"Is he married?"

She gave me a smug look. "Nope, he's single and available."

"How old?"

"Thirty-two," she said.

Mr. Ryan was a couple of years older than Mrs. Kirby. I would bet she'd rather be married to him than her squatty-body husband, El Stubbo. As always when thinking about Mrs. Kirby, I got distracted. While Mr. Ryan discussed our final project, I imagined her as I'd last seen her, arriving at Save 'n' Rave. I was heading out to take my break, unfortunately. Now I re-imagined the scenario. Instead of leaving, I ask if she'd like to join me for a cup of coffee.

"You drink coffee, Christopher?" she asks, looking surprised.

"I like it strong and black," I tell her. "Care for a cup?"

She nods and I beckon her to follow me outside. Strapped to my bike is an insulated pack holding a thermos of espresso. Mrs. Kirby lowers the rear door of her station wagon to make a seat. She sits, patting the space next to her. I grab the thermos and join her.

A fiery red sun is sinking behind the dumpster as we sip our coffee. There's only one plastic cup, so we pass it back and forth. Maybe it's the sharing that makes me feel close to her. Before long, I'm telling her about the custody battle. Mrs. Kirby listens, saying nothing. When I'm finished, she asks, "Who do you want to live with, Christopher?" I hesitate and she takes my chin in her hand. I'm forced to look into her swimming-pool-blue eyes. She repeats the question.

Maybe it's the strong coffee. In any case, I blurt out, "I want to live with you."

She sets the cup down and reaches for me ..... .

Now I stopped and shook my head to clear it. My daydream had galloped away with me. The scene I'd imagined didn't work on many levels. For one thing, there was my boss, the eagle-eyed Mr. Zagrobski. After ten minutes, he'd notice I hadn't returned from my break. He'd come looking for me. Seeing me sitting in the parking lot, he'd yell something like: "Koski, get your butt in here! You got a shipment of toilet paper to put away."

I had to come up with a better location. The Save 'n' Rave parking lot sucked as a private meeting place. I stared at the ceiling, thinking of alternatives. Then I remembered Bella Venezia, the small Italian restaurant on the next block. My dad took me there for my birthday. Unfortunately, he also invited Sherrie, who showed off, speaking Italian to the waiter.

The restaurant has tall, dark wooden booths that give you privacy. I imagined Mrs. Kirby and me tucked into a booth, out of the public eye.

We share a big platter of lasagna with extra cheese, sausage, and garlic bread. Mrs. Kirby pours wine from a straw-covered bottle. After we stuff ourselves with food, she pats the space next to her, saying, "Why don't you come over to my side?" I slide in next to her. We finish the wine and she turns to me. Her face is so close I smell garlic on her breath. She says, "You're a sophisticated young man, Christopher."

I shrug. "Chicks tell me that all the time."

Before long the restaurant's lights dim; it's closing time. Mrs. Kirby looks sad. I ask what's wrong. She says softly, "I wish I didn't have to go home. My husband is—"

I put my hand over hers. "You don't have to tell me. I know all about it."

As she dries her tears with a napkin, I throw a wad of bills on the table. Together we leave the restaurant. It's dark outside. I walk her to her station wagon. Before getting in, she takes my face between her hands and says, "This has been the best night of my life."

"Don't worry," I tell her. "There's more to come."

She drives away, a smile on her face. I watch until her car disappears. Then I go searching for my bike.

Now Shawna elbowed me, whispering, "Idiot, what are you smiling about?"

I sat up, blinking. "I wasn't smiling."

"You had a big, goofy smile on your face."

I wanted to tell her to MYOB, but Shawna's one of the most popular—and best-looking—girls in school. Instead, I focused on Mr. Ryan, who was wrapping up the discussion about our final paper. From what I gathered, we could write about any topic providing it was informative and he pre-approved it. I raised my hand.

"Yes, Chris?"

"Is it okay if we write fiction?"

He frowned. "Do you mean a manuscript?"

I wasn't sure what that was, but I said, "Uh-huh."

He raised his eyebrows. "No one's ever asked me

that. Let's discuss it after class, okay?"

My face was hot with embarrassment, yet I felt ten feet tall. *Mr. Ryan wanted to talk to me after class.*

Richie turned around in his chair. It wasn't easy because of his oversize body. He stared at me, his mouth stained purple from grape sour balls. "Have you lost your mind, Koski?"

"I've got a story I've wanted to write."

"I'll bet. You're just sucking up."

I took a deep breath, strongly tempted to answer, *Like the way you suck up food?* Instead, I ignored his remark, turning to look at the board.

Richie had a malfunctioning gland that made him fat. He claimed it was his family's genes; he inherited his size. Although that might be true, the kid did nothing to help himself. At lunch Richie was like a shark, circling the cafeteria tables for leftovers. His pockets bulged with bulls-eyes, gumballs, and Tootsie Rolls. He was an eating machine.

The bell rang. I shoved everything into my backpack. I had fifteen minutes to catch the bus that would drop me off downtown. Evan sprinted ahead, hurrying to meet his mom in the parking lot. I felt sorry for him. Although working at Save 'n' Rave is boring, it's not as bad as attending French class after school.

The lady who hands out free samples at the store gave me a ride home. I called Mom, saying she didn't have to leave work to pick me up. At home, I toasted a pair of blueberry Pop Tarts. Unfortunately, I was daydreaming. I burned them. I hate when that happens. The fruit drips inside the toaster, creating billows of black smoke.

While I was replacing the blackened tarts with fresh ones, the kitchen door burst open. Mom stormed inside, tossing her pocketbook on the kitchen table. That thing must have weighed fifty pounds. She collapsed into a chair and covered her face with her hands. After a while I said, "Mom, want a Pop Tart?"

In a muffled voice she said, "He's out to get me."

"Who's out to get you?"

"Your father. He's the devil's son."

I took a bite of Pop Tart. The hot fruit scorched my tongue. I grabbed a bottle of Mountain Dew and took a big swig. Then I carried the bottle and my plate to the table, sitting opposite Mom. "What's Dad done now?"

She shrugged off her coat. "He's taking out what's called a 'Complaint for Modification.' He's officially filing for custody." She got to her feet. "Mother of God, I need a drink. If you knew the kind of day I've had ..."

Mom dragged her chair to the sink. She climbed up on it to open the tall cupboard. My mother is short. I worry that I'll inherit this trait, the way Richie has inherited his family's fat gene. My pediatrician claims I'll soon be getting a growth spurt. I hope I grow tall, like my dad. If not, I've got a plan: I'm moving to Madagascar, where mysterious little people live in the forest, hiding in caves. I saw it on TV. None are over three feet. I'd be king.

I steadied the chair while Mom reached for a bottle of scotch. She climbed down and poured some in a glass, adding water and ice cubes. "You want a Coke or something?" she asked.

I raised my bottle of Mountain Dew. "Tell me about this complaint thing."

Before answering, she dug into her pocketbook and pulled out a pack of Marlboro Lights. "Do you mind if I smoke in the house this one time? I'm so upset I *have* to have a cigarette."

I shrugged. It wasn't the time to remind her that next week was her quit-smoking date.

She lit a cigarette and got up, opening the window over the sink. After taking a puff, she blew the smoke out the window. "Complaint for Modification means your father is legally attempting to change the custody agreement."

"We knew he was planning on doing that. What's different now?"

"What's different is that he's retained Spencer Thurston."

"Is he good?"

"Good? Spencer Thurston is one of the best lawyers in Boston. He could get Charles Manson elected to the school committee."

"Who's Charles Manson?"

"Never mind," she said. "Spencer Thurston is so good he's the Kennedy's lawyer."

"What about Mr. Farley? He must have a lot of experience, considering he's old."

"Mr. Farley's done real estate law for fifty years. This is family law. It's different." She took a gulp of her drink.

"Can we get another lawyer?"

She rolled her eyes. "I don't have the money."

"Would I have to talk to the judge, like on TV?"

She shook her head. "The court appoints someone, usually a therapist they're familiar with, to write a report on the parties involved."

"What kind of report?"

"The therapist interviews parents, family members, teachers, doctors. After gathering information, she makes recommendations." She looked at me critically over her glass. "When the therapist visits, you've got to be on your best behavior."

I was tempted to tell her the same. Make sure the therapist didn't show up on Saturday night when Mom and Doreen were partying in the den, blasting their lame music. Yet I said nothing. No sense in getting her upset. She had to hold it together. If not, I'd end up eating tapioca in the woods with my grandparents. Meanwhile, the nearest convenience store was three miles away. Granite Cove Beach was probably five miles.

During winter vacation I stayed overnight at my grandparents' house. After dinner we sat around like zombies, watching their ancient TV. Sherrie prepared "healthy snacks" in the kitchen (pineapple rings with low-fat yogurt sprinkled with coconut). Later, I helped get Gramps ready for bed. I held his dead arm while Gramma inched his pajama top over it. That night I heard coyotes howling outside. Down the hall, Gramps farted in his sleep.

Now Mom rested her feet on a nearby chair. She took a sip of her drink and sighed. "Your father is basically a jealous person. He hates that I've moved on with my life, while he's still living at home with his parents."

"If Dad is such a loser, how come you married him?" We had this discussion every time Mom drank scotch.

"He wasn't so set in his ways back then." She raised her eyebrows. "Did I ever tell you how I got my engagement ring?"

I shook my head, despite having heard it ten times.

Mom leaned back and gazed at the ceiling. "Your father and I had been going out for a year. On my birthday, he had a big night planned— dinner at the Parker House in Boston. I bought a gorgeous dress. I always tried to look nice. Matter of fact, I was chosen 'Best Dressed' in high school, along with 'Best Dancer.'"

"What was Dad chosen?"

"What?" Mom looked irritated at being interrupted. "I don't know, 'Class Nerd,' or something like that."

"That's a lie!" I slammed the bottle of Mountain Dew on the tabletop.

"Christopher, do you want to hear the story or not?"

"Yeah, but first tell me what Dad was chosen."

"Okay, it was 'Most Responsible.' Are you satisfied?" She didn't wait for my answer before resuming her story. "That night we were double-dating with another couple: Angela Halupowski, who was on the cheering squad with me, and her boyfriend, Skip Hogan, a running back for the Lobstermen. Between you and me, I always thought Skip wanted to ask me out. If Angie and I hadn't been friends, he would have."

"Would you have gone out with him?"

She looked pleased with the question. "I'll have to think about that one. *Anyway,* to make a long story short, on Friday afternoon I got a call from your father. He said he couldn't keep the date because he had to take his father to Nashua, or some godforsaken place, to buy a tractor, on sale. He acted like it was urgent. A tractor, can you believe it?"

I nodded, believing it.

"I was furious. I had to call Angela to cancel. She didn't like it one bit, not that I blame her. I was so mad I walked downtown, just to get out of the house.

I was looking at conditioner in the drug store when I bumped into Nicky Stubbington. Nicky's family had a summer place at Granite Cove Beach. That's where I met him, at the beach concession stand, where I worked one summer. I used to flirt with Nicky whenever he came in. He went to St. John's Prep and drove a silver 'vette."

"Do you mean a Corvette?"

"What else? Back then, a Corvette was the sharpest car on the road. Anyway, Nicky and I started talking, catching up. He said he was driving up to Hampton Beach to hear a band that night and asked if I wanted to go? Let me tell you, sweetheart, going to Hampton Beach in Nicky Stubbington's Corvette was better than dinner at the Parker House with boring old Roger Koski."

I sat up straight. "Dad wasn't boring back then."

"Trust me; he was boring at birth. Now let me finish." She stared out the window, a dopey smile on her face. "That night was a blast. We danced to every song. I'll never forget driving home on the shore road, listening to the Eagles on the radio."

I yawned. "What does this have to do with your engagement ring?" I knew the order of events. I also knew that my mom, once she got going, would drag out every detail. She's like a jeweler with his stones, polishing every facet until it shines.

"What happened was that Nicky and I were cruising the downtown, the radio blasting. It was spring. The night had gotten cold, yet we had the top down. When we stopped at a light on Main Street, I glanced at the other lane. There was a gray pickup truck next to us. I swear to God, you wouldn't believe who was in that truck."

"Who?" I asked, although I very well knew.

"Your father and his dad. Mr. Koski wore a plaid hat with flaps covering his ears. Inside the truck bed was a tractor. They looked like a couple of hicks from the sticks. I know they saw us, but pretended I didn't see them. When the light turned, Nicky peeled out, laying rubber all over the road." She threw her head back and laughed, reliving the memory.

I had to smile, guiltily, imagining the Corvette roaring away: *Up your exhaust pipe, losers!* "What did Dad say about seeing you with Nicky?"

"He never mentioned it. The following weekend he gave me a half-carat diamond ring from Blanchard's Jewelers."

"That's a funny story," I said.

"You think so?" She shook another cigarette from the pack.

I reached across the table, grabbing the matches. "Mom, remember what the court said about secondhand smoke, that's it's abuse? The judge won't let me stay if you don't quit."

I hated to ruin her good mood. Yet if she was going to quit, she had to start somewhere. It was time for tough love. Mom stared at me, her mouth quivering like a sad clown's. She released her hold on the matches. I put them in my pocket. Then I climbed onto the kitchen chair and put the scotch back in the cupboard.

FIVE

The following day I got home around suppertime. Doreen was sitting at the kitchen table, drinking a can of Miller Lite. Her head was covered with big hair rollers; this made her look like a giant ant. She gave me the once-over and said, "Hey, good-looking. Got a hot date tonight?"

"What happened to your head?" I reached in the fridge for the Mountain Dew. "You look like an ant-woman."

"Your mom set my hair. She says that when she's through I'll look like Julia Roberts."

I took a big gulp. "You'll look better than Julia Roberts." Mountain Dew always goes straight to my head. Not only that; I was in a good mood. Friday nights are a perfect time to visit Granite Cove Beach. Mom usually stays out late, which means I can stay out late too.

"Ginger," Doreen yelled to my mom in the next room, "your son is a real charmer. Who'd he get that from?" She snorted. "Certainly not from his dad."

Mom stuck her head into the room. "He probably gets it from my father. Remember what a flirt he was?"

"I'll say. That man could talk Mother Theresa into a hot tub."

"Dad flirted with everyone," Mom said. "Waitresses, teachers—even the census taker. They all loved him."

"Well, that's solved." Doreen rose and stood before the tall mirror hanging on the broom closet door. She turned slowly, staring at her reflection. "Ginger, be honest," she said.

"About what?" Mom, who was ironing nearby, didn't look up.

"About my butt. You told me it looked okay in these pants."

"Doreen, it looks fine. Will you stop obsessing about it?"

Doreen stared at her reflection. "It doesn't look fine. It looks huge. Let's face it: I shouldn't wear white pants." When Mom didn't answer, Doreen turned to me. "Be honest, Christopher. If you saw me coming into Save 'n' Rave, would you think, 'That lady has a big butt?'"

Mom stopped ironing. "For God's sake, Doreen. Chris is just a kid. Are you drunk?"

"I've only had two beers," she said. "Seriously, Christopher. You'd be doing me a favor. What do you think?" She turned around, her eyes closed.

I frowned, sizing her up. In tight white pants, her butt looked like the USS Constitution in full sail. Yet what I told her was, "If I saw you from behind, I'd think you were Julia Roberts."

Doreen hugged me, almost breaking a rib. "That's exactly what your grandfather would have said, God bless him. I'm sorry if I embarrassed you, Christopher."

I shrugged. "No problem."

Mom unplugged the iron and said, "Fold this up and put it away, will you, honey?"

I nodded. "You guys got dates tonight?"

"Doreen is fixing me up with someone named Eddie." She turned to Doreen. "Is he a good dancer?"

"How would I know?"

"I'm asking you because I know from experience that teachers are lousy dancers."

"Maybe grade school teachers are," Doreen said. "Eddie teaches high school. And who cares if he can dance, so long as he picks up the tab?" Doreen began unrolling the curlers from her hair, stacking them on the kitchen table.

I said I was going to get a start on my homework. Grabbing my books, I headed up the stairs to my room. Halfway up, Mom called to me: "I took a chicken pie out of the freezer. Can you heat it up okay?"

"No problem," I yelled back. I've been heating TV

dinners since I was ten years old, yet Mom still has to ask.

In my room, I didn't need to turn on a light. At this time of year, the daylight never seems to end. When darkness creeps in, it's so slow you can't tell at what point day turns to night.

I tossed my books on the floor and flopped onto the bed. Resting my chin on the sill, I looked out the window. Thin bands of purple stretched across the sky, melting into a pink sunset. Across the street, the empty lot was bursting with trees, shrubs, weeds, and vines. In June, fireflies flickered among the tangled vegetation. I'd often thought the overgrown lot would make a great setting for a sci-fi movie. When I was a kid, I used to stare out the window, waiting to spot a UFO.

As Mom and Doreen got ready downstairs, I worked on my project for Mr. Ryan's class. I'd decided to plot my story beforehand. It was Mr. Ryan's suggestion, to create an outline. "You wouldn't set out on a journey without a map," was how he described it.

Before long, I heard Mom and Doreen in the hallway downstairs. It sounded like they were getting ready to leave. I heard Doreen say, "I'm only staying for a couple of drinks. I've had a long day."

Mom replied, "I can't stay later than ten. I don't want to leave Christopher alone too long."

They always had this conversation before going

out, yet when the Ship Ahoy announced closing time, they were still there. Sometimes Mom called to say she was "on her way," although something always kept her. It wasn't like they were a couple of booze hounds, glued to their seats. It was more like they bumped into old friends; suddenly they were in high school heaven. Days later, they would still be talking about seeing that old classmate. You'd think they'd met in the jungles of Borneo instead of the local hangout.

At the door they argued about who was going to drive. Finally, they decided it was Doreen's turn. Mom yelled goodbye to me. I yelled back. The door slammed shut. I raced down the stairs.

In the kitchen, the smell of perfume was so strong I had to open a window. I decided to put the chicken pie in the microwave instead of the big oven, to speed things up. That was a mistake. When I took it out, the crust was stiffer than the carton it came in. I hid the mess in the trash. I wasn't hungry anyway. I was never hungry before visiting Granite Cove Beach. Besides, surveillance is best on an empty stomach.

Finally, I headed out on my bike. It was getting dark; the passing cars had their headlights on. After two miles I approached the faded wooden sign: "Granite Cove Beach, Private Way". I made a right and soon found myself clattering over the rutted road which ran behind the cottages.

I ditched my bike behind a tangle of wild rose

bushes. As I walked down the road, I checked out the cottages. Most were dark, but that wouldn't last long. After Memorial Day, the summer residents returned, on weekends. More people meant more chances of my being noticed. I had to face the inevitable: My visits to Granite Cove were numbered.

When I was below the Kirby cottage, I worked my way up the sandy embankment. At the top, I crawled through the tall, wet grass. It tickled my nose. I made note of the time: nine fifteen. As I got settled, the porch light went on. I ducked my head so fast I got sand in my mouth.

It was Mrs. Kirby, standing under the yellow porch light and holding the screen door open. She wore jeans and a striped rugby shirt. A second later, Butchie waddled out on skinny, stiff legs. Going down the steps, the old dog looked like a marshmallow on four toothpicks. When he reached the bottom, Mrs. Kirby went inside, leaving the porch light on.

I held my breath as Butchie waddled over to the grass beyond the cement path. There he squatted to take the longest pee I'd ever witnessed. When he finished, he lumbered back up the steps. At the top, he barked shrilly. The porch door opened. Mrs. Kirby, glasses perched on top of her head, appeared. I smiled.

After Butchie disappeared inside, I watched the living room window where Mrs. Kirby sat. The light from a standing lamp fell on her shiny, dark hair. A few seconds later, El Stubbo appeared and stood in my line of vision. "Move, lard-ass," I muttered. It was so annoying, like being at the movies and someone with an enormous head sat right in front of you. I wished I could throw something at the window to get him to move. He was probably complaining that dinner had given him gas. He was so gross. One night he sat in the chair Mrs. Kirby's sitting in and clipped his disgusting toenails.

Poor Mrs. Kirby. I wanted her to know she wasn't alone. I closed my eyes and sent her a message: *Angel, someone is watching out for you.*

While waiting for El Stubbo to move, I rested my head on my arm. I was shocked to discover I'd dozed off. When I woke, it was cold. Only one light was on at the Kirby house. What had awakened me was a persistent tugging on my leg, accompanied by a low growl. I rubbed my eyes and stared at the source of the noise. It was a nightmare: Butchie was in the act of pulling my pants off!

I shook my leg. "Quiet!" I hissed, but he wouldn't stop. He must have remembered me from the last time. Now the mutt was primed, his gray muzzle clamped like a vise on the hem of my jeans. Kicking my leg made him growl louder. Throwing sand made him pull harder, ripping the material with the strength of a pit bull. How could such an old dog be so strong?

The front porch light went on. My mouth went dry when Mrs. Kirby called, "Butchie! Butchie!" I thought I'd pee my pants. I had to escape before she went looking for him. I rolled toward the dune. The old dog hung on, rolling along with me. He wouldn't release his death grip on my jeans. I, on the other hand, wasn't going to stick around. Over the dune we went, like two logs cascading down a waterfall.

At the bottom, I shook my leg like crazy. It made him pull harder. One second later, I heard footsteps on the porch. I considered my options. I had two choices:

1.) Arrive home with an ancient beagle attached to my pant leg.

2.) Lose the jeans and lose the dog.

I chose number two. With trembling fingers, I pulled off my sneakers. Next I fumbled with the buttons on my jeans and peeled them off, aided by Butchie.

"There, ass-wipe," I hissed at him. "Take them."

Despite his spindly legs, the old dog scrambled up the dune, my pants dragging behind him in the sand. At the top he paused to shake his prize, clamped in his muzzle. Then he trotted away, tail held high.

I didn't stick around. Tucking my shoes under my arm, I ran barefoot and bare-legged, passing rows of cottages until my lungs felt ready to explode. Near the end of the beach I finally collapsed on the front steps of a darkened cottage.

After my breathing returned to normal, I headed for my bike. Upon reaching it, I wondered what I should do. How could I ride all the way home in my BVDs? Not only that, I had sand up my butt and my legs were freezing. After thinking about it, I decided what to do. I took off my jacket and t-shirt. Then I stuck one leg at a time through the arm holes of the t-shirt. It helped that it was an old, stretched-out shirt. Gathering the material, I knotted it at my waist. Fortunately, it was a dark night. If a passing car spotted me, maybe they'd think I was a yogi wearing a loincloth.

Finally, I put on my jacket and zipped it to my chin. My poor legs, jammed inside the arm holes of my t-shirt, had zero circulation. They felt as cold as popsicle sticks. My testicles were so numb I was afraid they'd snap off. Yet I was able to ride away, a little wobbly at first until I got used to it.

Luckily the shore road had little traffic. I sat hunched over the bars of my bike, pumping my legs up and down. When I finally neared my street, I relaxed a little. At that point I was so cold I didn't notice the car. It arrived quietly, slipping in next to me, slowing down to keep pace. Out of the corner of my eye I spotted the big gold seal on the cruiser's door: "Town of Granite Cove Police Department."

At first, I ignored the car, staring straight ahead. Then I glanced over to nod at the two cops watching me. I turned my attention back to the road until I was caught in a flashlight's beam. "Pull over, kid," someone said.

I stopped and shielded my eyes from the glare.

"What's your name?" the one in the passenger seat asked.

"Christopher Koski."

The cop behind the wheel, an older, beefy guy, asked, "Your old man own the hardware store?"

"That's right."

He chuckled. "We played hockey together. Your old man's one tough SOB on the ice." The other cop, his face expressionless, said nothing.

I leaned down to look in their window. To the fat cop I said, "Thanks, Officer. I'll tell my dad. Can I go now?"

"Chris, tell us where you're headed and where you've been."

"I'm going home to one twenty-seven Neptune Street."

"Now tell us where you've been tonight in your underwear. Do you know it's ten forty?"

"Really? Oh, no; I'd better get home. My mom'll be so worried."

"You haven't told us where you've been."

"I was swimming at Granite Cove Beach."

"Water's pretty cold this time of year, ain't it?"

"A little, but I don't mind."

"Chris, come over here and empty your pockets."

I dropped my bike on the ground and approached

the cruiser, reaching into the pockets of my jacket. My heart was thudding so loud I was sure they heard it. At the same time I was thankful I had nothing from the Kirby's clothesline. How would I explain a pair of black silk panties?

I pulled a tube of Chapstick and half a pack of Skittles from one pocket. The cop aimed his powerful flashlight beam on them. Next, I reached into the other pocket. I fished out a wad of tissues and an unwrapped bulls-eye candy covered with lint.

"That all?" the fat cop asked.

"Uh-huh."

"Okay, turn your pockets inside out."

I did as I was told, standing there while they looked me over.

The younger cop asked, "You have any drugs on you?"

"No, sir. No drugs." Where would I hide them, I wondered, in my butt?

He nodded. "Now ride your bike to your house and we'll follow. We want to have a word with your parents."

Although it was cold out, my face got hot and sweaty. "Uh, my dad doesn't live there, and my mom's probably on an errand." I added, "She'll be back any minute." The Ship Ahoy bar closes at midnight. Maybe by some miracle Mom left early.

They didn't cut me any slack. "Let's check, then; see if she's home."

With that, they eased the cruiser ahead, leaving me no choice but to follow on my bike. The ride down my street was *the most* embarrassing moment of my life. There I was, half-naked, a cop car creeping alongside me. The only thing worse would be them turning on the siren. When we passed Alyssa Putnam's house, I prayed she wouldn't be looking out the window. If that big-mouth saw me, it would be all over the school by Monday.

When I pulled into our driveway, Doreen's car was gone. I doubted if Mom was back. The only light inside the house was the one I'd left on, above the sink. That meant Mom was still out. I dropped my bike and the cops pulled up behind me. I approached them, feeling naked in the glare of their headlights. "My mom's probably at that twenty-four hour place getting groceries."

They exchanged glances. "She do that a lot? Leave you alone nights?"

"Officers, I may look young because of my height, but I'm fourteen." They continued to stare, their expressions unchanged. I tried again. "My mom goes to the Kwik-Pik when we run out of juice." I shrugged. "She's afraid I'll get scurvy, or something." I smiled but they didn't smile back. "She's coming right back. I'll have her call you as soon as she gets home."

The fat cop sighed. "Son, put your bike away. Then you go inside and get dressed. Leave your mom a note saying you're at the station. We'll wait for you."

"What?" My voice was a squeak. "I can't do that. Listen, Officer, my mom's coming home. She ... she's a slow driver."

"Would you rather we take you to your dad's? Does he live in Granite Cove?"

I shook my head. "No, you don't need to do that. Um, why don't I go inside and call my mom?"

"You know where she is?"

I didn't want to tell him she was at the Ship Ahoy. While I stalled for an answer, he said, "Chris, listen to me. You're a juvenile, out late at night, in your underwear and unsupervised. We can't leave you alone. Suppose you're on drugs, you burn the house down? We'd be responsible. Now, when your mother comes home, she can pick you up at the station. So get dressed. Bring your homework or whatever, and don't forget to leave a note."

I nodded, totally depressed. "Okay, Officer, but if you write a report, don't call it my underpants. I'm practicing to be a yogi and this is, like, my uniform."

He glanced down. "Looks like underwear to me."

"Well, it's not," I said, frowning. "I wear this when I do yoga on the beach."

The cop nodded. "Fine. Now hurry up, because we don't have all night."

I felt like I was starring in a reality TV cop show. For a moment I feared I was going to cry. Instead, I turned and ran into the house. While inside, I thought about locking the doors and hiding in the cellar. I had a perfect spot, behind my grandfather's old Army locker. At the same time I pictured the beefy cop busting down the door. When they took me out, handcuffed, the neighbors would be gathered on the lawn, silent and staring. Alyssa Putnam would take photos to show everyone at school.

After putting on a pair of jeans and grabbing my book bag, I combed my hair in case they took mug shots at the station. I tried a couple of tough looks in the mirror, reminding myself to not smile.

Downstairs in the kitchen, I scribbled a note:

> *Dear Mom,*
>   *How are you? I am fine.*
>   *When you get home, please pick me up*
> *at the police station.*
>   *Love,*
>   *Christopher*

I searched through the phone book for the police station's number. My eyes kept blurring with tears. In the end, I threw the book on the floor. Let Mom find the number herself. If she'd been home, the cops wouldn't be hauling me away. This would never happen to Evan. His mother might be a douchebag, but she'd never put him in such a situation. It was the worst night of my life, and I blamed my mom and Butchie.

I finally left the note on the kitchen table and went outside to the waiting cruiser.

SIX

I studied the details of the police station so I could write about it later. Mr. Ryan encouraged his students to keep a journal, write it all down. I didn't think he meant the Granite Cove police station, but who knew?

On the outside it looked like an old red-brick building, the kind you'd see in any small town. On the inside, it was a futuristic cube with panels of blinking lights and automatic doors that silently slid open. Around the main desk was a cluster of four tiny closed-circuit TVs showing what was going on in the jail cells. Tonight they were empty except for one; it held an old guy who snored really loud. The young cop called him "Clayton."

I sat on a bench near the door, eating gluten-free pretzels from a vending machine. Not a donut in the whole place, unfortunately. The fat cop had gone back. The younger, red-haired one stayed behind, relieving the desk cop. He gave me a body-building magazine someone had left behind. After a while, the old guy woke up and cried, blubbering into his hands.

"Keep it down, Clayton. Your lawyer is on his way to post bail."

The old guy stopped and stared at the ceiling. Then he swung his feet to the floor and sat up, blinking. He wore a fancy striped shirt that hung out of his pants. His white hair stood in spikes all over his head. He asked, "Do you mind telling me why I am here?"

"DUI," the cop said without looking up.

"How can that be? I wasn't driving."

"You were driving, Clayton."

He shook his head. "No. It's all coming back to me. I needed a rest and I stopped. I definitely wasn't driving."

"Technically no, but the motor was running," the cop said, "with you behind the wheel. That's considered driving in Massachusetts."

"Now you listen to me. I was not driving that car."

"Tell your lawyer. He's on his way to pay your bail."

"What about my daughter, Pamela? Did anyone call her?"

"Uh-huh. She told us to call your lawyer."

He puckered his mouth. "Is that so? Maybe when I change my will she'll wish she hadn't."

"You keep hiring Spencer Thurston, there'll be nothing left in your will."

"You shouldn't have bothered Spencer," the old man said, yawning.

"Would you rather spend the night here?"

He looked around and spotted me. "Hello, young man. Were you also driving while intoxicated?"

I shook my head. "I don't have my license."

"I don't either. The coppers keep taking it from me." He laughed at this, slapping his leg.

A moment later the outside door opened. A man in a long black coat, white scarf, and shiny black shoes appeared. He looked like a character in a play by Charles Dickens. All he needed was a shiny top hat. He approached the automatic doors.

The cop looked up. "Mr. Thurston, I'll buzz you."

The doors slid open and he entered, smiling. "Thanks, Denny. Has my boy been giving you any trouble tonight?"

"He's been sleeping it off. We found him near the boulevard slumped over the wheel of a leased Jaguar. The vehicle was in park; the engine was running. He was combative and refused a breathalyzer."

"Is that right?" He turned to the old man. "Clayton, are you ready to go?"

The old man stood, unsteady on his feet. "Now listen to me. I never drive and certainly not at night."

"Well, somebody did," the lawyer said. "Are you ready to leave?"

The guy struggled into a tweed sport coat he'd balled up and used as a pillow. "You're in evening clothes," he said, glancing at the lawyer. "Did I take you away from a party?"

"We were at the ballet. Frankly, I welcomed the chance to escape, if only for a moment." He added, "Marjorie is at home."

"Don't keep the dear girl waiting. Officer, open this door immediately."

"Simmer down, Clayton," the cop said. "Your attorney has to fill out some paperwork." He handed the lawyer a clipboard with documents attached. Spencer Thurston gave me a brief nod before joining me on the bench. I watched from the corner of my eye as he scanned the printed sheets. With wavy silver hair, he looked like a ship's captain. Watching him, I suddenly connected the name, Spencer Thurston, with his occupation: lawyer. My stomach clenched. *I was sitting next to my dad's custody lawyer!*

I raised the magazine and hid my face, pretending to read. A moment later, a loud clattering sounded on the stairs. When I looked over, Mom stood at the entrance. Her black mascara was smeared. Peering through the metal bars of the electronic door, she looked like a trapped raccoon.

"Oh my God," she wailed, upon spotting me. "*My son is in jail!*"

I stood, dropping the magazine on the bench. "Hi. I'm ready to go."

The cop asked, "Is this your mother, Chris?"

"Uh-huh." I was tempted to add "unfortunately," but didn't.

When the doors slid open, Mom raced in. She threw her arms around me like I'd been abducted. I pulled away. "Mom, let's go home, okay?" I glanced at Spencer Thurston bent over his report. "We'll talk outside," I said, taking hold of her arm.

"Ma'am, I'd like to see some identification before I release your son," the cop told her.

"Of course." She fumbled in her bag, yanking stuff out before handing him her license.

Returning it to her, he said, "I smell alcohol on your breath, Ms. Koski. Did you drive over here?"

"No, my girlfriend drove. She's outside."

The cop handed the license back. "Your son is not to blame. We found him out late on his bike, in his underwear. He said he'd been swimming at Granite Cove Beach. That's dangerous for anyone, alone and at night. Naturally, we first suspected drugs—"

"Drugs!" She stared at me, bug-eyed.

"Ms. Koski, please listen. We didn't find drugs, but we were concerned. Your son was out late, unsupervised. When we discovered no one was home, we brought him here."

She stared at me and cried, "Oh, Chris, haven't I been through enough?"

"Mom, let's go." I tugged on her sleeve, dragging her along before she could say anything else. The cop buzzed the door. Before heading up the stairs, I looked back. Spencer Thurston had stopped writing and was watching us.

Outside, a light mist filled the air. "Where's Doreen's car?"

Mom pointed across the street but made no move to cross. She reached for me, clutching my shoulders and peering into my face. With her makeup smeared by tears, she looked like a demented clown. I hoped no one from my school was driving by to witness my humiliation. She said, "Whatever happened tonight, Christopher, you are not to repeat a word to your father. Do you understand?" She shook me to emphasize her point.

"Don't worry," I said. "I won't." My dad would hear about it soon enough from his lawyer.

We crossed the darkened street. Mom got in front with Doreen while I climbed in back. The minute she buckled her seat belt, she began sobbing and telling Doreen every detail. "Honest to God, you have no idea what it's like, seeing your only child behind bars. All I could feel was failure—my failure as a mother. Is it because I'm a single parent? You know I never wanted the divorce. I was willing to make it work. This is all Roger's fault."

Doreen agreed that it was my dad's fault. "Women are always blamed and it's the woman who has to pay, Ginger, one way or another."

Mom blew her nose. "Sometimes I think it's that terrible music the kids listen to, the F-word all the time. We never used that word when we were teenagers. My parents would have kept me in for a month if they'd heard me say that. Now I hear it everywhere, even on public streets."

"Kids today have no respect," Doreen said. "It shows in how they dress. Girls wear their skirts so short you can practically see their you-know-whats."

"And they don't care if you do," my mother answered.

The two continued to discuss the sorry state of young people today. They didn't ask to hear my side of the story: What *was* I doing in my underwear at night? Didn't they want to know? Any issue that Mom can't understand she blames on the divorce. She couldn't see that she and Dad weren't meant for each other. His idea of a fun night was pricing tires at Sears and then stopping for fried clams. He even brought his own tartar sauce because Bob's Clam Shack charged extra for it.

Mom's idea of fun was inviting her high school friends to the house to dance and drink. The talk and the music got louder as the night went on. Poor Dad was out of his element with that crowd. To make matters worse, Mom never missed an opportunity to make fun of him. At her parties, she'd say, "Roger, can you smile? You look like you've been sucking lemons all night." Everyone would laugh. They'd tell Mom she was a "scream." At ten o'clock, Dad headed up to bed while the guests were rolling back the rug to dance. "He's so square," she'd announce when he left. While Dad snored upstairs, Mom was downstairs showing off her dance moves.

Now, while Mom and Doreen complained about my generation, I dozed. When I opened my eyes, we were on Neptune Street. The maple trees were lacy with new leaves. It reminded me of how, when spring arrived, my family used to go for walks after dinner. Dad had carried me on his shoulders. I'd had to duck when we approached a low-hanging maple. I'd felt like a king, sitting up high, smiling at the neighbors.

Despite all that happened later—the fighting and accusations—we were once happy. All you have to do is look at our family album. There we are in photos, smiling and unaware that our world would soon shatter. It was like we'd lived inside a glass snow globe. One day a giant picked it up, shook it, and destroyed everything.

Thursday night rolled around. That meant dinner with Dad at my grandparents' house.

"Christopher, would you like more haddock?"

"No thanks, Grams."

"Why? Don't you like it?"

"I do, but I've had a lot." I patted my stomach to demonstrate.

"Haddock is over ten dollars a pound," she reminded me.

Knowing the price of haddock wasn't going to make me any hungrier. During Thursday night dinners at my grandparents', I try to act more mature than I really am. I always feel like I'm on display and being judged. Basically, they're looking for evidence of Mom's bad influence. Now I looked across the table at my dad, who seemed distracted and hadn't said much all night. Even when he'd picked me up after work, he'd been quiet. I hoped his silence didn't have anything to do with my night at the police station. He couldn't have gotten word that soon. On the other hand, maybe his lawyer hadn't realized I was his client's son. I might have gotten away with it if Mom hadn't gone in and created a scene.

As if reading my thoughts, Grams said, "Roger, you're awfully quiet tonight. Don't you feel well?"

"I'm fine, Mom. Just tired."

"How's the new bookkeeper?" she asked. "I hope she's not one of those girls who spend all their time putting on lipstick and talking on the phone."

Sherrie appeared from the kitchen, carrying a plate of French fries. Normally that was my favorite food, yet not the way Sherrie makes them. Her French fries are mushy. She said to Grams, "Don't worry. I'm helping to train the new bookkeeper. She's a nice person. Evenings, she volunteers in the hospital's chaplains program."

Sherrie placed the fries in front of me. She sat next to Dad, putting an arm around the back of his chair. I bit into a fry. It was tasteless and as soft as mashed cauliflower.

Gramps, who'd paid attention to Sherrie's remarks, said to Dad, "You're lucky to have a smart girlfriend."

"Oh, Pops," Sherrie said, blushing and beaming.

I looked down at my plate, knowing where the conversation would lead. His remark about Dad's "smart girlfriend" was a veiled dig at my mom. What Gramps meant was: *not like your former wife*. My grandparents are too impressed with Sherrie. They love that she teaches math at the Good Shepherd School, a Christian high school.

Sherrie must be a mind reader. She looked across the table and asked me, "Did you remember your algebra homework?"

"Uh, no. I forgot."

Dad scowled at me. "Sherrie was good enough to offer to help you, Christopher. At least you could remember to bring it."

I stared down at the pale, soggy fries. "I'm sorry, Sherrie."

She reached over the table to muss my hair. I tried not to cringe. "I know you'd rather write your stories," she said. The way she said *stories* made it sound like writing was a nutty hobby. Like those people who stuff and mount dead pets.

To change the subject, I said, "Dad, do you like the new bookkeeper?"

"I do. She'll help with payroll, keep the books."

Gramps, whose eyes were at half-mast, said, "I

hope she's prettier than the pointy-nosed woman who visited us last week."

"That was Dr. Hutch," Dad said, glancing at me. Somehow I knew he was referring to the therapist assigned to the custody case. I reached for the ketchup bottle and poured more over my soggy French fries.

"She was a nervy thing," Grams said.

"What's 'nervy' mean?" I asked, desperate to change the subject.

"It means she asked questions that are none of her business. Imagine wanting to know if your grandfather and I slept in the same bed. That woman doesn't know her place."

"What'd you tell her?" I asked.

"I said it was so dark when I got into bed I had no idea who was there."

Dad cleared his throat. "Dr. Hutch asked those questions because it's part of her evaluation."

Gramps pushed his plate aside and hoisted his arm on the table. It made a big thud. I stared at it, noticing how the fingers on that hand were curled like a claw. I swallowed hard and looked away.

Gramps said, "She doesn't need to know who we sleep with. All she needs to do is look around, to see how we live. No one smokes or drinks. We're good American people." At that, he looked over at me. I knew the meaning behind his words: We're not like your mother.

Grams said, "What is this country coming to when perfect strangers come into your home and ask questions your best friend wouldn't ask?"

"She never asked me anything," Gramps said, sounding disappointed.

"She did, but you're so deaf she got tired of asking."

"Good," he said, "because I got nothing to say. What kind of wacky doctor is she, anyway?"

"She's a psychologist with a family practice," Dad said.

I couldn't stand hearing another word about Dr. Hutch. I jumped to my feet and scooped up dirty dishes. My hands full, I scurried to the kitchen to avoid what I feared would follow: a discussion about the custody case.

Grams told me to sit. There was tapioca pudding for dessert.

"I have to go to the bathroom," I called, shoving dirty dishes onto the counter. I scooted past the table and ran up the stairs. No one called me back. If there was one thing that was sacred in my grandparents' house, it was a visit to the bathroom.

Upstairs, I shut the door and leaned against it. I didn't really have to go. I just wanted to escape the conversation. To pass the time, I opened the medicine cabinet. It held the same old bottles with yellowing labels: witch hazel, calamine lotion,

Preparation H, Pepto Bismol, and laxative tablets. As I examined each, I couldn't stop thinking about the conversation downstairs. Dr. Hutch, the court therapist, had visited my grandparents' house. That meant she'd soon be coming to my house.

It felt like the walls were closing in on me. I shut my eyes and leaned my forehead against the cool glass of the cabinet door.

Outside, an animal shrieked. I opened my eyes; my pupils were huge. If I lived in their house, I'd never get used to the night sounds. Not only that, I'd become "peculiar," a word Gramps uses meaning weird. That can happen to those who live in the woods. I imagined it happening to me: after a while I wouldn't notice the vines creeping over the windows, shutting out the light. I'd become a hermit, staying inside to brood. Eventually I'd have to go downtown for supplies. The old-timers who sit on the bench in front of the post office would say, "There's the Koski boy. He used to be an okay fella till he went to live with those old folks in the woods ..."

Now I ran water into the rust-stained sink. I washed my hands with a new bar of Sweetheart soap. Its flowery smell reminded me of Mrs. Kirby. I closed my eyes, but instead of imagining Mrs. Kirby, I felt the shame over what had happened that afternoon at the store ...

I'd waited until her cart was half-full before approaching near the dairy section. "Hi, Mrs. Kirby.

Let me know if you need any bags of dog food from the back. I'll carry it out for you."

Instead of thanking me, she covered her face and cried. It was a shocking sight: Mrs. Kirby standing in front of me, sobbing. El Snotto stuck his thumb in his mouth. He stared at his mother, looking ready to start bawling himself.

"Wait," I said and sprinted down the next aisle to paper goods. I grabbed a box of tissues and returned. Opening the box, I was clumsy. When I tried to grab a few, the whole wad flew out. It lay in clumps on the floor. I scooped some up and stuffed tissues into both her hands and El Snotto's. This made him cry. I stood there, hands in pockets, hopping from one foot to the other.

Finally, Mrs. Kirby dried her eyes. She picked up the kid and bounced him a little. "I'm sorry, Christopher," she said, putting a hand on my shoulder. "It was the mention of dog food. You see, we've lost Butchie."

"Butchie's ... lost?"

"He—he died." Her lips quivered but she didn't cry.

I stared at her, dreading what she'd say next, that Butchie had choked on a pair of boy's jeans. Finally, I managed to croak, "What happened?"

"Old age, probably. He was thirteen. His heart gave out."

I mumbled something about being sorry. "I'd better get back."

I raced off to the employees' bathroom, where I stared into the cracked mirror. My mind was spinning like hamsters in a wheel. Had I caused Butchie's death? If so, could I face Mrs. Kirby again?

That night, on the ride home from dinner, Dad turned the radio to a jazz station. Mom had never let him listen to jazz while she was in the car. "You call that music?" she'd complain. "You can't dance to that." His silence was making me nervous. I suspected what it was leading up to: a heart-to-heart talk.

My suspicions were confirmed. Before the approach to Neptune Street, he pulled over to the curb and shut off the engine. Oddly enough, it was the same spot where the cops had stopped me for riding in my underwear. I stared straight ahead, dreading the inevitable.

He let out a sigh. "Son, we're both tired, yet I want to tell you something."

"Yeah?"

"I don't want you to worry about the current situation."

"I'm not worried, Dad."

He looked over at me. "I'm talking about the custody case."

Hearing the words "custody case" made me feel a little sick. However, I looked straight ahead and replied, "I'm not worried because my mind is made up. I want to live in my own house, where I grew up."

I added, "It's only normal."

He was quiet for a moment. "Listen, son, I don't want to play the bad guy role. But you've got to accept that as a parent I know what's best in this situation."

"Dad, I'm happy where I am. If I had to live with my grandparents, I'd hate it. At my house, everything is nearby: my school, my job, my friends—"

"That's another issue, school. We're very lucky to have Sherrie. She's mentioned you to the headmaster at Good Shepherd. Do you realize they have a long waiting list?"

"That Jesus school? You gotta be kidding."

"That's a false impression, son. I visited the school last week. I was very impressed. The students get an excellent education. In fact, the older kids are taking calculus." At that, I lowered my window to get some air. He continued, "At this point in your life, you don't realize how important school is. But let me tell you, today's colleges are super-competitive. Students need advanced skills that you won't get at Granite Cove High—"

"Dad, I'm only fourteen. I'll worry about that in a couple of years."

He reached over and patted my head. "Trust my experience, Chris. I know it's hard to accept, but—"

"I might be young, but I know my own mind. Give me credit for that."

He was silent for a moment. "Remember not long ago when you needed braces, and you refused them? You put up such a fuss, but we didn't back down. If we'd given in, you'd have crooked teeth today. Instead, you have a beautiful smile."

"This is different, Dad. Besides, my English teacher thinks I'm a good writer. That's what I want to do, not math. Not only that, I'm not religious."

"There's little religion at Good Shepherd, and not all its students are Christians. Instead, they have something called 'ruminations.' Students share their thoughts about a parable, not necessarily from the Bible." He added, "Sherrie says it's very popular."

Ruminations, I thought. The word made me think of cows in a field, mindlessly chomping grass. Instead of answering him, I opened the car door. "Are you going to drive me home or should I walk?"

He started the car and I closed the door. We drove in silence until we reached my house. He pulled into the driveway but didn't go all the way in. His hands clutched the steering wheel. Then he turned to me. "Son, I *hate* disrupting your life. I hate the mess of a custody fight. Do you think I enjoy this? Please understand I'm doing what is best for you."

"Dad, it's not best for me." I looked at him. "Honest, it's not."

In the dashboard light he looked old. Deep lines were etched across his forehead. "Someday you'll understand and you'll thank me. Right now your future is at stake. Your mother refuses to see it."

"Okay, this is what I have to say: If the judge makes me move, I'll run away."

"Don't talk like a child."

"Don't treat me like a child."

"If you remain with your mother, you'll have a police record by the time you're sixteen. I can't sit back and let that happen."

I felt my face growing hot. He obviously knew about my visit to the Granite Cove police station. He started the engine. "I have to help the folks get ready for bed. We'll talk again."

"Okay, but I hope you heard what I have to say. If they make me leave home, I'll run away."

He shook his head wearily. "It sounds like your mother's been putting ideas in your head."

I wrenched open the door handle. "No one puts ideas in my head. No one but me!"

With that, I ran into the house. When he pulled out of the driveway, Dad didn't flash his lights or beep his horn.

SEVEN

The next morning, Mom came downstairs wearing her old quilted bathrobe. She stared at me across the kitchen table. Her face looked puffy, like she'd been crying. "I'm going to make coffee. Do you want eggs?"

"Huh?" It was weird, Mom being downstairs so early. I usually have the kitchen to myself. "I've got Froot Loops," I said, pointing to my bowl.

"That's not a healthy breakfast."

"It's fine." I didn't mention that Froot Loops were what I ate every morning. She'd know that if she bothered to get up early. Instead, I said, "I love Froot Loops."

She wasn't listening. She said, "I woke up and thought, why not take the day off? Holy Moses, I deserve it. Yet if I stayed home, I'd do nothing but worry about Dr. Hutch and her upcoming visit."

"She's already gone to Dad's house," I told her.

She raised a hand. "Don't tell me."

"Don't worry, Mom. It'll work out okay."

"Oh, Chris." She took a wadded-up tissue from her pocket and pressed it to her nose. "How can you say that?"

"It will, Mom. Don't start crying. I talked to Dad last night—"

"You did? What'd he say?"

"I told him I was happy here and hated the idea of moving to my grandparents' house."

"How did he take it?"

"We kind of left it up in the air. I think he's considering it."

"God, I hope so. I just want it to be over with—the therapist's visit, the judge's decision." She leaned across the table and kissed my cheek. "I'd better take a shower. Thanks for the talk, hon."

Before she left the kitchen, she looked back at me. I gave her a thumbs-up. She gave me a lopsided smile. My mom needed to hear upbeat news. It didn't matter if it came from a fourteen-year-old. She'd convince herself it was true. In some ways, she was like a kid herself.

Before I left to catch the bus, I took a big swig of warm Mountain Dew. At the door, I paused to burp. It was so long and so loud I might have set a record. Too bad there was no one around to time it.

In English class, Shawna Curran helped Mr. Ryan pass out forms. He said, "These are permission slips to attend the Student Essay Reading at Addison

College in Boston. I've nominated four essays, including three from this class." He glanced my way. "Every year I take my freshman class to the reading. I expect all of you to attend. Afterward, I want you to write about the readings—which essays made an impression and why."

Vinnie stared in disbelief at his form. He turned to Richie, sitting next to him. "If he thinks I'm gonna waste a Friday night listening to a bunch of jerk-offs read, he's dead wrong."

"Hey, Vinnie," Richie said, "maybe you and me can sit together on the bus. Afterward, we can go to Peking Palace."

Vinnie stared at him. "Blubber boy, do you think I'd be caught dead eating won ton with you?"

Richie shrugged. "I got a gift certificate for my birthday. It'd be free."

Vinnie gave him a disgusted look and slumped deeper in his chair. Richie turned to Evan and me. "You guys wanna go to Peking Palace that night?"

Fortunately, we didn't have to come up with an answer. Mr. Ryan began talking about our next assignment: Write about an event that made such a strong impression that it created an insight. "Otherwise known as an epiphany," he said, looking around the room. "Can someone tell me the meaning of 'epiphany?'"

Shawna raised her hand. "It's when you're surprised about something. It's like a moment of truth."

"That's good, Shawna—a moment of truth. Have any of you had such a moment?"

Alyssa Putnam, the class know-it-all, raised her hand. "I had one, Mr. Ryan. It was last summer when my grandmother had a gallbladder operation. My family was sitting in the waiting room and when her doctor came in, I had a terrible thought: *What if my Grammy dies?*"

He nodded. "I don't want to rain on anyone's parade, but death comes to us all. No one gets out of this world alive." He rubbed his palms together. "Okay, about this assignment, I want you to think about something life-changing. When and how did you have your epiphany?" He looked around the room, his expression stern. "Give the subject some thought. Don't write it off the top of your head. Let us feel the impact."

I wrote the assignment in my notebook, wondering what was *my* moment of truth? Was it the moment I fell in love with Mrs. Kirby? I gnawed at my thumb. There was no story in that. Mrs. Kirby hardly knew I was alive. If only I could write a scene the way I *wanted* it to happen. I stared at the blank pages of my notebook. The lines blurred as I felt myself sliding into a daydream:

Despite the warm spring afternoon at Granite Cove Beach, few people were around. I walked barefoot on the smooth concrete boardwalk, my fishing pole resting against a shoulder. My sneakers, tied together, hung from the other shoulder. I looked out at the wild surf. It was a perfect day for stripers.

As I neared the creek with its jutting rocks, I heard a scream. I stopped to scan the shoreline, shielding my eyes from the sun. About twenty yards from the shore, I spotted someone thrashing around in the wild surf.

Tossing my fishing pole aside, I tore off my clothes, leaving only my white BVDs. I climbed over the railing, pausing to look down at the twelve-foot drop below me. Without hesitating, I leaped through the air and landed on all fours. Once on my feet, I charged into the waves. The drowning victim appeared tired from struggling. He or she was going down for the last time.

I hurriedly swam to the spot where I'd last seen him or her. Reaching underwater, I managed to grab a fistful of hair. I tugged the swimmer to the surface. It was Mrs. Kirby who emerged from the churning surf, sea water streaming from her face. She gasped and cried, "Christopher!"

"Don't talk," I ordered, circling her torso with my right arm. Using the cross-chest carry, I towed her to shore. Before we could reach it, we got caught in a riptide. We were carried for several yards until I could resume swimming.

Finally, we reached shallow water. I carried her, staggering, onto the beach. At that point I noticed *that she wore a leopard-print bikini. When we reached the hard sand, I set her down and straddled her lifeless body. Her eyes were closed. I shouted, "Mrs. Kirby, can you hear me?"*

I covered her mouth with mine and began basic rescue breathing; I'd learned it at camp. After a minute she coughed and opened her eyes. Looking up at me in wonder, she whispered, "Christopher, you saved my life."

"It was nothing, Mrs. Kirby. I happened to be nearby."

We gazed at each other. Mrs. Kirby's eyes were as blue as the lake at Camp Pesquasawasis, where I'd learned the cross-chest carry along with basic rescue breathing.

"You're the bravest boy I know." She reached up and pulled me toward her ...

My dream ended when Evan poked me with his elbow. I blinked and looked up, feeling dazed. Mr. Ryan stood at our desk, giving me a questioning look. "I asked for last week's essay on disappointment. Do you have one, Chris?"

"Yeah." Quickly I flipped open my binder. I showed him the essay, feeling the eyes of the class on me.

He looked at it briefly and nodded. "Can I see you for a minute after class?"

"Sure."

SHARON LOVE COOK

I felt my cheeks burning. Did Mr. Ryan think I was sleeping? Would he say something to Dr. Hutch when she interviewed my teachers? "Chris doesn't seem to get enough sleep," he'd tell her. She'd nod.

When Mr. Ryan moved on, I glanced at Evan. He shrugged and rolled his eyes.

Richie turned to Vinnie. "This assignment sucked. I couldn't think of anything disappointing to write about."

"Oh, really?" Vinnie said. "How about the time you went to that all-you-can-eat buffet and they ran out of food?"

"Huh?" Richie scratched his head. "That never happened."

"It's a joke, blubber boy. It'll happen one of these days, the way you stuff that pie-hole of yours."

"Where's your essay?" Richie said.

Vinnie leaned back in his chair. "What is this, kindergarten? I got better ways to waste my time."

Mr. Ryan must have heard Vinnie. He turned back, stopping at Vinnie's desk. "Where's yours, Madruga?"

"I dunno," Vinnie said. "Let me find it."

He stood and slowly searched his pockets, one by one. From a shirt pocket he withdrew a crushed pack of cigarettes and tossed them on his desk. Finally, he took out a multi-folded sheet. Taking his time, he unfolded each tiny square. "I was gonna write about the night I was brushing my teeth in the dark. I used jock-itch cream instead of toothpaste." When the class laughed at this, Vinnie looked around, grinning.

Mr. Ryan scanned his paper. "Do you want to share this with the others?"

"Not hardly," Vinnie said.

"That's fine, if it's personal."

"It ain't that. I wrote about how one night I stood up to my old man. I was waiting for him to take a swing at me." He shrugged. "I guess he was scared. He never laid a hand on my mother or me again."

Mr. Ryan nodded. "You've had to be a tough guy, is that right?"

"Yeah. What's wrong with that?"

"Nothing wrong with that. Have you ever heard of the writers Raymond Carver or Raymond Chandler?"

"Nope."

"I think you'd like them. They write about tough guys."

"Tell you the truth, I don't like to read. Waste of time."

After class, Evan said he'd wait outside while I met with Mr. Ryan. That didn't sound like Evan. I think he was just nosy about why Mr. Ryan wanted to see me. I told him I'd be right back, leaving him in front of my locker. Then I entered Mr. Ryan's classroom. When I approached his desk, he pulled out the chair next to it. "Am I holding you up, Chris? Should you be somewhere right now?"

"It's okay," I said. "I'm not working this afternoon." I sat and attempted a smile, trying to appear casual, though my left knee was bouncing like a jackhammer.

"Chris, I'll start by saying how impressed I was with your essay on the family. When you wrote about walking home in the snow after Midnight Mass on Christmas Eve, I was touched. It's a very moving account, and I'm recommending it for the Addison College student essays. The best writers from the Boston area high schools will be reading their work."

"Mr. Ryan, you mean it? I'm going to read in front of all those kids?"

"Your essay will be an excellent addition," he said, "along with another member of this class. But you need your parents' signed permission before I can submit it." He handed me a form from a folder on his desktop.

While I looked it over, the door that connects the rooms opened. Ms. Carbone peeked around the corner. "Hi, Rob. You busy?" She smiled, showing all her teeth like an alligator.

"I'm tied up now, Grace-Ann. I'll drop by when I'm through here."

She winked, withdrew her head and closed the door.

Grace-Ann, I thought, a dumb name that suits her. Wait till I tell Evan. I stuffed the form into my backpack. "I'll go now, Mr. Ryan."

I started to rise but he put a hand on my shoulder. "Just a moment. What were you saying the other day about the final assignment?"

"Um, I asked it's all right if I make it fiction."

"All of my students are doing a report format, but that's not cast in stone. We can be flexible. Personally, I think it's great you want to try fiction. Do you have something in mind?"

"Yeah. It's a story I've been thinking about for a long time. It's too long for a short story and too short for a novel."

"Do you mean a novella?"

I nodded, not sure what a novella was but willing to agree to anything. I couldn't believe Mr. Ryan was listening to me talking about my writing and taking me seriously.

"What's it about?"

"Um, it's about a kid from Yugoslavia who flees to the US with his family ..." I stopped in case he didn't want to hear any more.

"And? Can you give me a run-through?"

I took a quick breath. "My main character's name is Boris. He's my age. He's got a mother and father, a sister Sonya, and dog, Tonka. When they lived in Yugoslavia, they were very rich with a big mansion and plenty of servants. In fact, one of the servants did nothing but squeeze the toothpaste for family members."

Mr. Ryan chuckled. "That's really rich," he said.

"War breaks out and the family has to flee. Before they do, they take all their millions from the bank. They convert it into precious jewels and have them sewn into Tonka's dog collar. Eventually they make it to this country. Their first night in New York City, they get a room at a fleabag hotel. Because they don't speak English, they wander around looking for a place to eat. They go into a diner, but the cook yells at them for bringing their dog inside. They're forced to leave Tonka tied up outside.

"Later when they leave the diner, they discover Tonka is missing. Was he stolen? They search frantically, calling his name in the streets. They eventually return to their hotel, heartbroken. Not only have they lost their dog, they've lost their fortune (the jewels, remember, were hidden in his collar).

Now they can't pay their hotel bill and they get kicked out. They move to a rooming house in the most dangerous area. Boris's father, who used to be an aristocrat with royal ties, now works as a janitor. Boris's mother, who had a chauffeur to drive her everywhere, now gets paid to do people's laundry. Boris and his sister collect cans and bottles from the streets.

The family, who once hired private chefs, now eats beans from a can. Not only are they poor—with no TV—they're sad, having lost their dog." I stopped and glanced at Mr. Ryan. "That's all I've written so far."

He whistled. "You have a wonderful and colorful imagination. That's something that can't be taught." I thanked him and got to my feet. "Keep working on your story," he said. "I want to hear more."

Evan was in the corridor, leaning against my locker. He looked up. "You look like you've just visited Santa Claus."

Feeling confident after my talk with Mr. Ryan, I ignored his remark. "Don't you have French lessons this afternoon?" I asked, needling him.

He wasn't listening. His attention was focused elsewhere. "Koski, act natural," he muttered. "Sno-Cones Carbone is heading our way."

Sure enough, the lipsticked barracuda was heading toward us, swinging her hips. She wore a tight pink sweater tucked into a tight skirt. Her high heels made a loud clacking sound on the hardwood floor. She probably realized that Mr. Ryan wasn't going to return her visit, so she decided to track him down. He's too nice to tell her to "get lost."

Suddenly overcome with embarrassment, I pulled the permission form from my pocket. I pretended to study it, my face burning like I'd smeared it with Louisiana hot sauce. Evan, however, sauntered casually. As we passed, she gave us a look like we were something she'd wiped from the bottom of her shoe. When we'd gone a few yards, Evan whispered, "She knows we talk about her."

"All the guys talk about her," I said. "And by the way, she's on her way to see Mr. Ryan."

"Yeah, you notice how she throws herself at him?"

"Mr. Ryan's a serious writer. He's got better things to do."

"Koski, that's lame. You sound like a middle school nerd."

"What do you mean?" Evan's always insulting me. I rarely defend myself because most of the time I'm afraid he's right.

Evan stopped. "Hey, think about this." He held up both index fingers and moved them far apart. "What if I stood at one end of the corridor and Sno-Cones Carbone stood at the other?"

"Yeah, so what?"

"We run toward each other fast as we can, and collide in the middle." He gave me a questioning look.

"Yeah, what about it?"

"Do you think her Sno-Cones would make indented cones in my chest?"

I pretended to think it over. Finally, I said, "There's only one way to find out."

"You arrange it, now that you're buddy-buddy with Ryan."

"No way, numb-nuts."

Evan grabbed my arm and spun me around like we used to do at grade school recess. I was a lightweight then. He could practically lift me off my feet. This time, however, my arm slipped from his grip. I slammed into the lockers. It made a loud crash and just about knocked the wind out of me. We laughed so loud that Mr. Dunbar, the principal, stuck his head around the corner. He glared at us. When we finally calmed down, Evan said, "Koz, you were asking me earlier if I had French lessons after school."

"Yeah, how come you don't?"

"For your information, my mom has jury duty. I am officially free."

I stared at him. "Do you mean—"

He nodded. "Uh-huh, we can play Phone Freaks at your house."

"Awesome, dude." We high-fived each other. "Quick, let's run to the bus," I said. We raced each other down the corridor to the exit doors.

EIGHT

We got off the school bus at the convenient mart. There we bought candy, something Evan's not allowed at his house. Then we walked the quarter-mile to my house. I'd forgotten how much fun it was being with Evan. We laughed over the same stuff. For instance, while we were approaching my street, a father and his kid passed us on bikes.

They wore matching yellow plastic helmets. The father's bike was turquoise, with flower decals like a girl's. He sat up straight in his seat, his elbows sticking out like Mary Poppins. When he passed us, Evan turned and followed, imitating the guy's jutting elbows, his skinny nose stuck in the air. (Evan's a great mimic.) The father must have sensed someone behind him; he turned around, fast. His bike wobbled and he let out a screech as he toppled onto the dirt. The kid laughed, and we did too. In fact, we practically peed our pants, running all the way to my house.

Inside the kitchen, I poured us glasses of Mountain Dew. Then I heated some frozen mini-pizzas. We sat at the breakfast table and had three each.

"I can't believe Mr. Ryan is going on the field trip," I said.

Evan shrugged."He has to, doesn't he? He organized it."

Evan doesn't like me talking about Mr. Ryan because they're not buddy-buddy. Mr. Ryan is polite to Evan, but kind of distant. Unlike the rest of our teachers, he's not impressed with Murray. For some reason this makes me like the guy even more.

When we finished the pizza, I set my glass down on the table. "Murray, are you ready to play Phone Freaks?"

"Dude, I'm ready."

"Wouldn't it be awesome to call Ms. Carbone?" I said. "We can pretend we're Mr. Fontaine, and say he's sweet on her."

"Sweet on her?" he repeated. "Where'd you hear that one?"

"My grandmother. She always asks if I'm sweet on anyone." I wrinkled my nose.

"Why don't you freak her out and say you're sweet on Stefan, the foreign exchange student?"

I laughed and shook my head. "My grandparents couldn't handle that."

"Old people are weird. Does your grandfather still have that arm?"

"What do you think, it fell off? Of course he has it."

"No offense, Koz, but it's kinda creepy."

"Well, what's he supposed to do, cut it off?"

"Hey, man, don't get your panties in a twist. I was only kidding. By the way, are you still spying on that old lady?"

I felt my face getting hot. "She's not an old lady, and I'm *not* spying."

"Okay, let me put it another way: Are you still observing that older woman at Granite Cove Beach?"

I shrugged. "I sometimes go over there."

"Koz, I can tell you're mad. I'm just curious; that's all. I mean, you're my best friend. I don't want to see you get into trouble."

Sometimes I wish I'd never confided in Evan, telling him about Mrs. Kirby. Our friendship had always been like that, me telling him everything while he says little. "I don't intend to get in trouble. I only go over there for a half-hour, at night. I hide in the tall grass and watch her."

He raised his eyebrows. "Watch her doing what?"

"Doing dishes, stuff like that."

"Dishes? That sounds really exciting. You're telling me you ignore Shawna Curran for some ... woman ... who doesn't know you're alive?"

"What do you mean about Shawna? She doesn't like me."

"You are so lame, Koz. Shawna likes you. A blind man could see that."

"Shawna's crazy about Mr.Ryan," I said.

"Every girl in our school is crazy about Mr.Ryan, including Mr. Ryan."

"How come you don't like him?"

Evan shrugged. "He thinks he's so cool with his long hair and sports jackets."

"Nah, that's not true," I said.

"Whatever you say. You're so sweet on the guy you won't listen to *any* criticism." He held up a hand. "Let's not talk about Ryan. I want to hear what's so special about this Kirby lady. What does she look like? Maybe I'll come with you some night."

"Your mother won't let you," I reminded him. Not only that, bringing Evan would violate a major rule of surveillance. It's an activity best performed alone.

Although I felt self-conscious, it was nice to talk about Mrs. Kirby to someone. I stared down at my plate as if I could see the answers there. "What does she look like? She looks like Snow White, from the old Disney movie. Her voice sounds like tinkling bells. When she approaches me at the store and asks, 'What's the special today, Christopher?' I feel like I'll melt into a puddle. I just like to be close to her. If I can't be close to her, I like to be nearby." I forced myself to look at him. "I'm aware that it all sounds lame."

He shrugged. "Well, you always were a little ... different."

I'd gotten carried away and had said too much.

Now I leaped to my feet. "I don't know about you, but I wanna play Phone Freaks."

"Let's do it."

We moved into the TV room where I handed him the spare copy of the Granite Cove phone book. Sitting on the floor, we silently scanned the pages in search of good—meaning weird—names. "Don't call out just any name," he said. "Wait for the perfect one to find you."

"I know the rules, butt-breath," I said, slowly moving my finger down the columns of names.

As it often happens, Evan was the first to find a good one. He laughed and rolled on the floor, hugging the phone book to his chest.

"Hey, jerky," I said, "this had better be good."

He sat up and wiped his eyes. "Christopher, lad, I believe I have found a perfect specimen."

"Don't be such a dick. Tell me."

"Are you ready for this?"

"Quit busting my—"

"Chester Dolby."

I let out my breath, considering his find. "Oh, man, a true freak. How do you manage to always find them?"

"It's a special talent I have, inherited from my great-grandfather."

"Really? I didn't know they had phones way back then."

"No, dummy. He found a life preserver from the

Titanic, washed up on shore."

"Awesome, man. You mean it washed up on Granite Cove Beach?"

He shook his head. "It was on Prince Edward Island, where he lived. He kept it for years. My parents don't know what happened to it. Imagine what it'd be worth today."

"Wow. I'd love to see it. That's so awesome."

"Maybe some day I'll work for the FBI's freak investigation unit," he said.

"How do you look at a name and right away know it's connected to a freak?"

"Simple. If your parents named you Chester, wouldn't you turn out a little strange?"

"You've got a point, Special Agent Murray."

"Do you want to call Mr. Dolby?" he asked, being nice.

I sighed. "I'd like to, but I can't sound *mature,* like you."

"One of these days you will," he said, tapping in the number.

I waited, holding my breath as the phone rang. It went unanswered for a long time. Evan looked at me and shrugged. He was about to hang up when he gave me a thumbs-up. "I'm going upstairs," I whispered.

I took the steps two at a time, racing into my mom's room. I leaped on her bed and grabbed her pink princess phone on a night table. I was just in time to hear Evan ask, his voice respectful, "Excuse me, is this the home of Mr. Chester Dolby?"

"That's right. Who's this?" Mr. Dolby was loud. For some reason folks with weird names tend to talk loud.

"This is Frederick Krueger with the Granite Cove phone company. I'm checking your telephone line."

"Why? What's wrong with it?"

"Mr. Dolby, would you look out your window and tell me if your line is securely connected to the telephone pole? We've had complaints that there's a disconnect in your area."

Mr. Dolby sighed. "I'm gonna have to go upstairs to the front bedroom to see the line."

"That's fine. I'll wait."

Mr. Dolby muttered something and noisily set the receiver down and stomped off.

"Evan, you're a genius," I whispered into the phone while Mr. Dolby was gone.

"Wait for more," he whispered back.

After a long wait, Mr. Dolby returned. "It's all balled up so's I can't tell. What in blazes am I looking for, anyway?"

"What's that, sir? You say the line is balled up?" Evan's voice was low.

"Yeah. Now that you mention it, I can't hear you very good either. You said something's wrong outside?"

"I did, sir. I'll report this to your area supervisor. We may have to send the de-balling unit over there.

Now, will you please check one more thing?"

"If it's outside, you'll have to do it yourself," Mr. Dolby said. "I've got bad knees, and I pretty much stay put."

"No, sir. This can be checked inside."

"Yeah? Well, what is it?" The old guy sounded cranky, like Gramps.

Evan spoke rapidly, running his words together: "Would-you-please-conduct-a-wiener-check?"

"A what? Don't talk so fast. Say that again."

"A wiener check, Mr. Dolby. Would you kindly check your wiener?"

Mr. Dolby swore and slammed the phone down.

Later we went over every bit of the conversation. Because Mr. Dolby had been such a perfect phone freak—"a classic"—we decided to stop there. "Anyone following him is bound to be a letdown," Evan said. I recorded Dolby's name in a secret notebook so that we didn't duplicate future efforts.

After that, we headed to the kitchen. Although it wasn't cold out, I made cocoa the way we always liked it, with three melted marshmallows per cup. While I heated the milk at the stove, Evan looked at the photos and stuff on our refrigerator door. He zeroed in on a white appointment card.

"Hey, Koski, what's this? You've got an appointment with Dr. Vivian Hutch, youth and family counseling."

I winced. Evan *would* spot that. He's always

sniffing things out, especially the secret stuff. On the other hand, it's hard keeping things a secret when your mom posts it on the refrigerator. I decided it was time to mention the custody fight. When I finished, he said, "You mean you might have to live with your dad at your grandparents' house?"

I nodded, stirring the pot faster. "I won't live with them, because I'll run away. I've already decided."

"Hey, Koz, if you run away, I'm going with you."

"I appreciate that, man. But just think what would happen if you came along. Within an hour your picture would be on every milk carton in the country. Even if we snuck on a ship to Russia, Evan Murray's face would be plastered on Russian milk cartons." I poured the cocoa into mugs and carried them to the kitchen table.

"You could be right," he said. "What's this therapist going to talk about?"

I shrugged, tiring of the discussion. "She'll probably ask about my home life, about my mom. Stuff like that."

"What'll you say about your mom?"

"I'll make her sound like *your* mom."

"How's that?" he said, licking melted marshmallow off the spoon.

"You know how your mom is. When you're in the bathroom for more than two minutes, she bangs on the door, wanting to know what you're doing in there."

"She's afraid I'm exploring myself."

"You probably are, you perv."

"My mom sent me to a shrink once." His tone was casual but he glanced quickly at me.

"She did? I didn't know that."

"It was embarrassing," he said. "I didn't want anyone to find out."

"I always tell you when stuff happens to me."

"It was at the beginning of the school year. Richie Digou talked me into hiding in a stall in the girls' room." He grimaced. "We got caught."

"You and Richie, together in one stall? Impossible." I laughed. "Who caught you?"

"Alyssa Putnam. We were standing on the toilet seat. When she came in, he got all nervous. His foot slipped into the toilet. She started yelling. We only went in because the floor had just been washed and the door was wide open. I went along with the dumbass prank because I felt sorry for Richie."

"What happened?"

"The school counselor contacted my parents, who sent me to a shrink. They were afraid I was developing 'unwholesome tendencies.'"

"I'm mad that you didn't tell me," I said. "Some best friend you are."

"I'm sorry, Koz. I just wanted to forget it. If that wasn't bad enough, Ms. Carbone urged Alyssa to file a charge for sexual harassment. I hate Ms. Carbone."

I nodded, smiling to myself. Knowing that Evan

did dumb things made me feel better. "You want more cocoa?"

"No, I've got to start walking. I wanna get back before my mom gets home." He stood for a moment, paused, and sat down. "I just thought of an awesome idea."

"Yeah? What's so awesome?"

"It's the answer to your custody situation. When you hear it, you'll thank your stars for having such a brilliant friend."

"So tell me," I said.

He cleared his throat. "When you're talking to the shrink and she asks why you don't want to live at your grandparents, tell her you have reasons. You don't want to talk about it because it's personal. She'll try to pry it out of you. Finally, you say you'll tell her providing it's confidential. You say you don't want to live at their house because your grandfather has, you know, *inappropriately* touched you." He winked at me. "You know what I mean."

I stared at him, too shocked to speak. Was he kidding?

He leaned back in his chair. "So, am I a genius?"

When I didn't reply, he continued, "It'd work, you know. The courts hear stuff like that all the time. And best of all, your grandfather wouldn't know what you said. It's privileged information, between you and the shrink. Whatever you say to them is private. The end result is that your dad loses the case. It's history."

"Except for one thing," I said.

"What's that?"

"It's a lie. My grandfather would never do anything like that. It's too sick to even think about." In fact, it was. My stomach felt queasy.

Evan leaned forward. "So what? Do you realize they're going to march your sorry butt out of *your own* house? You'll live in the sticks with coyotes. You'll wear farmer overalls. You'll have cow crap on the soles of your shoes."

"Murray, you're definitely a genius, but I can't do that. I'll think of something else."

He stood and drained his mug. "Don't say I didn't try to save you." He crossed the room and without a word, headed out the door.

"Thanks for coming over," I called to his retreating back.

I moved to the door and watched Evan crossing the lawn. When he reached the sidewalk, he broke into a run. I waited for him to turn and wave, but he didn't. I closed the door and carried the pot to the sink. As I rinsed it out, I thought about his idea, lying about my grandfather in order to save myself. It occurred to me that Evan would do such a thing to save himself. He was my best friend, yet I hardly knew him anymore.

The next afternoon I got out of Graphic Design class early. On impulse—if you call something you've planned an impulse—I stopped by Mr. Ryan's classroom. He was sitting at his desk, writing. Hovering over him, her chest practically resting on his shoulder, was Ms. Carbone. She saw me first, looking at me like I'd crawled out of a slime bog. I would have vanished right then if Mr. Ryan hadn't spotted me. "Hi, Chris. What's up?"

"Excuse me, Mr. Ryan. I don't want to bother you, but I have a quick question."

He glanced up, exchanging a silent message with Ms. Carbone. She said, "I'll catch you later, Rob." With that, she turned and walked to the connecting door, her butt moving like a sack of jackrabbits.

He motioned me into the room. "Have a seat, Chris."

As soon as I sat, I felt embarrassed. Was I being a pest? Was Mr. Ryan merely tolerating me? He may have sensed my doubt because he leaned back in his chair and said, "You ready to tell me more about your manuscript?"

"I'm going to work on it this weekend," I said. "I was wondering if you have any books about writing that I could borrow."

"I've got shelves of books about writing. Let me look through them. I'll find a couple that would appeal to where you are now in your writing."

That made me feel like a real writer. I got to my feet. "Okay. Thanks, Mr. Ryan."

He looked surprised. "Do you have to go now?"

"Uh-huh. I work after school at Save 'n' Rave market."

"Good for you. Keep notes of your impressions working there. Believe it or not, you'll often refer to this period in your life."

It was hard to believe that years from now I'd be writing about stocking shelves with adult diapers and mousetraps. Nonetheless, I nodded.

"Work on the manuscript," he said. "Write a little every day, even if you don't feel like it."

"I always feel like it."

"Excellent. So many writers drag themselves to their desks."

"Really?"

I couldn't imagine not wanting to write about my characters. Although they were made up, they were real to me, as if they lived in my head. Every time I wrote, I discovered more about them. It was like I was channeling Boris and his family. They speak to me; they come alive through my pen.

During break time at Save 'n' Rave, I went to the loading dock. There I watched the guys who drive the big rigs. Sometimes I helped them unload, although not the heavy stuff. Sometimes they give me a couple of bucks.

The drivers are from all over the country. I love imitating the Southern accents. They, in turn, imitate my "New England" accent. "I don't have an accent," I said. It made them laugh. When they weren't aware

I was around, I listened to their dirty jokes. At night, I recorded them in my notebook, like Mr. Ryan suggested.

I was about to go back inside when I spotted Mrs. Kirby's car entering the parking lot. I ran to the employees' bathroom and rinsed out my mouth. From my pocket I dug out a breath mint.

After exiting the bathroom, I headed up aisle number two. Mrs. Kirby was at the front of the store, heading toward me as I knew she'd be. Her kid sat high on a booster in the shopping cart. He wore a tiny denim jacket. His shiny hair was cut in a bowl-shape. El Snotto's got one of those freckled, cute-kid faces that you want to smack. Mrs. Kirby, on the other hand, looked like a model in a magazine, selling Sweetheart Soap.

"Hello Mrs. Kirby," I said. "Can I help you with anything?"

"Thanks, Christopher." She smiled at me. "You can help me decide what to have for dinner tonight."

"We've got a sale on loins." I quickly added, "*Pork* loins."

I felt heat rising from my neck. Sometimes it went all the way to my ears, turning them pink. The word "loins" hung in the air. What a dumb thing to say. Maybe she thinks I'm a smart-ass. To cover my embarrassment, I patted the kid's head. He batted my hand away.

"I'll check it out," she said, moving on. "Thanks for the tip."

"Um, how's the charcoal holding out? Want me to get some out back?"

"We're okay for now, Christopher. But thanks for asking."

I stood there, a sickly smile on my face, as she moved away. My face was probably as red as a watermelon. I raced back to the employees' bathroom and splashed cold water on my cheeks. As I dried my face with a paper towel, I took slow breaths, closing my eyes. I would use my imagination to change the terrible, awkward scene I'd just experienced. When I felt calmer, I pictured Mrs. Kirby leaving the store. While driving home, she can't get me out of her mind:

Later, when I got out of work, it was dark. I spotted a familiar station wagon parked in the rear of the lot. In the moonlight I could make out a shadowy figure in the front seat. The car's headlights flashed, beckoning me. I moved toward it in a trance. As I got closer, I heard music coming from the radio, a sax playing something low and sweet.

Mrs. Kirby sat behind the wheel, her eyes closed, her head resting against the seat. In the moonlight her lipstick shimmered. She opened an eye and smiled up at me. Her dress made a swishy sound when she reached forward to take the keys from the ignition. She tossed them at me. "Here, you drive."

I was jolted from the daydream by a loud pounding on the door.

"Hey, lemme take a whiz, will ya?"

I opened the door a crack. It was one of the truck drivers. "Whatsa matter, kid, you fall in?"

"Sorry." I lowered my head and scurried away.

"Thought you died in there," he called after me.

NINE

I arrived early at computer class and sat at my desk, daydreaming about Mrs. Kirby, something I find myself doing a lot. As Shawna Curran passed my chair, she punched my arm. "Cut it out," I said, rubbing the sore spot where she'd hit me.

"Sorry, Christopher. I thought you were in a trance."

It's hard to stay mad at Shawna, who's pretty and knows it. "Forget it. I owe you one."

She twirled a long strand of blond hair and said, "You can pay me back at Evan's pool party next week. Wanna hang out together?"

"Pool party?"

Her cheeks turned pink. "Um, maybe you didn't get your invitation yet." She glanced across the room. "Here's Evan now. You'd better check with him." With that she scurried to her desk.

Evan, spotting me talking to Shawna, immediately looked guilty. When he reached our shared desk, he tossed his books down and turned to the windows. "Do you think Fontaine would have a cow if I opened a window? It's hot in here."

Evan looked uncomfortable. I decided to ask him point-blank. "Shawna told me about a pool party you're having. She wondered why I hadn't gotten my invitation."

His laugh sounded like a seal's bark. "Pool party? Last night it was sixty degrees. Does that sound like pool weather?"

Without waiting for a response he moved to the window. As he struggled to open it, Mr. Fontaine appeared and glared at him. "Young people, how many times must I tell you not to touch the windows! This room is climate controlled." When Evan skulked back to his seat, he said, "Open your textbooks to chapter six, 'The Information Highway.'"

Evan, looking contrite, leaned toward me and whispered, "Can you come to my house after school?"

I nodded. "Yeah."

One way or another, I'd get the truth from him.

The Murrays' house was on a winding street where all the homes were similar: split-level ranches in different colors. The Murrays' was the neatest, freshly painted with windows that sparkle. Their lawn is like green velvet, not a dandelion in sight. Mr. Murray must shave it to get that smooth surface. The family van is also immaculate. Mr. Murray washes it every weekend. His routine involves getting down on his knees to scrub the tire crevices with a toothbrush. While this is going on, Mrs. Murray, the barracuda, yells orders from the window: "Don't forget to use Glass Wax on the chrome!"

A bumper sticker on the back of their van proudly claimed: "My Child Got Top Honors at Granite Cove Middle School." That child was Evan's younger sister, Katrina. She was "gifted" and got A-plusses in every subject. Without a doubt, Katrina was the Sister from Hell.

That afternoon, when I rapped on the front door, the little genius herself answered. She gave me a look like I was wearing dirty underwear. "What do *you* want?"

"Evan around?"

"Unfortunately, Evan's always around." She continued to stare at me through her pale eyelashes. Katrina's skin is so white her veins show. She wears her white-blond hair in a long fuzzy braid.

I leaned against the door. "Can I come in?"

"Not if I have anything to say about it." Nonetheless, she turned and shouted to Evan.

A moment later he poked his head around the door. "Hey, Koski, come in, man."

"What are you juvenile delinquents plotting?" Katrina asked with a sneer.

Evan took her place at the door, forcing her

against the wall. "Katrina, screw, okay?"

"I'm telling Dad." She ran off.

Evan and I smiled at each other. "Wanna ride bikes?" I asked.

"Can't."

"How come?"

He looked away. "My dad wants me to show him how to do something on the computer."

"I can wait."

"Nah, it'll take too long." He continued looking past me.

Evan had brought me all the way to his house for nothing. "Okay, then," I said, crossing my arms over my chest. "You wanna tell me about the party you're having next week?"

Before Evan could answer, Mr. Murray appeared. He wore a white shirt and, over that, a navy vest with a pocket that held pens. He had a sour look, like he'd been sucking lemons all day. In all the years I'd known the Murrays, I'd never seen his dad smile. Now he poked Evan's chest with a bony finger and said, "Did you just say the f-word to your sister?" Behind her father's back, Katrina stuck her tongue out at Evan.

"No," Evan said. "I told her to screw."

Katrina bounced up and down. "He said the f-word! Evan said the f-word!"

"Quiet, Katrina," Mr. Murray snapped. To Evan he said, "We do not use that language in this household. You're staying in this afternoon. Tell Christopher he has to go."

Evan turned to me, rolling his eyes. "Sorry, Koz. Maybe tomorrow."

Mr. Murray, hovering in the background, piped up. "Tomorrow you have science club. Then your mother's taking you shopping, remember?"

I turned away. "See you around, Murray," I said, letting the screen door slam behind me. Walking to my bike, I felt like a stray dog banished from their doorway. I hopped on my bike and drove zig-zags over their perfect lawn, hoping Mr. Murray was watching. As I rode down their street, I tried to ignore the ache in my throat. I'd had what Mr. Ryan would call an epiphany: Evan, my best friend, was turning into his dad.

Now I pedaled harder, refusing to waste tears on the Murrays. I thought what I could do to retaliate. If I'd had a lot of money, I would have hired a plane to fly over their house and drop a ton of dog crap on their roof. Nothing would make me happier.

My situation improved considerably when I got home. Mom announced that she was going out that night. "It's a cosmetics party," she said. "It's like a housewares party, only instead of plastic containers, they sell makeup. One of the girls from the registry of deeds invited me." She added, "Don't worry. I won't be away long."

"Take your time," I told her. "You deserve it."

She smiled at me from the stove where she stirred frozen chicken and noodles, a glass of wine in her hand. I told her I'd eat later; I had a lot of homework to finish. I raced up the stairs. It was true when I said I'd eat later—when I returned from Granite Cove Beach. A surveillance professional doesn't work on a full stomach. He might fall asleep.

After about thirty minutes, Mom yelled goodbye from downstairs. I waited for the sound of her car backing out of the driveway. Then I slammed my book shut and leaped off the bed. I'd already slipped into my dark jeans and hooded navy sweatshirt.

Before long, I was pedaling on the shore road. The air smelled salty and from far off I heard the surf. The moon above was a thin crescent offering little light; in other words, perfect conditions for surveillance.

After turning into the beach road, I was whizzing along, passing the rows of darkened cottages. Yet even from my vantage point, I noticed changes. The shutters were removed from a few houses. Ladders were propped against the wood-shingled exteriors. Boats sat exposed, their tarps removed. I drove past a speedboat with the dumb name of "My Sanity" and a rowboat with the cool name of "Ship 4 Brains."

The telltale signs indicated that summer was coming. From June to September, Granite Cove Beach would be overrun with residents and tourists. My nights of lying in the grass, undetected, were coming to an end.

After ditching my bike behind the boathouse, I skipped up the sandy steps to the boardwalk. I ran along the smooth concrete, watching the moon's shimmering reflection on the water. When I reached the appropriate spot, I followed the wooden-slat path, stopping at the foot of the dune. Taking a deep breath, I climbed up, grabbing clumps of wet grass along the way. At the top I lay flat and slithered through the tall beach grass on elbows and knees. When I reached my observation spot, I lay still, letting my heart slow to normal.

My efforts were rewarded with the sight of Mrs. Kirby at the sink, washing the kid's hair. When she poured water over his head, he shrieked. She sang a song to distract him. It was a "spider" song I remembered from nursery school and I silently sang along. Mrs. Kirby followed with another tune. I closed my eyes, tucking my chin into my cupped hands. The singing continued ...

I must have dozed off, because I was abruptly yanked awake. Someone gripped the hood of my sweatshirt, forcing me to my feet. I twisted around to see who had me. It was Mr. Kirby, his face in shadow as he gripped my hood. "What are you, some kind of pervert?" he muttered. "What's your name, kid?"

I opened my mouth. Nothing came out except a croaking sound. I'd awakened to a real-time horror show.

"Come inside," he said, yanking on my hood and

pulling me toward the cottage. "Maybe you'll talk to the cops."

"Mr. Kirby," I managed to say, my mouth as dry as the sand beneath us.

He peered at me. "How do you know my name?"

I forced myself to look at him. Through chattering teeth I said, "I know Mrs. Kirby."

As if on cue, the porch door opened. "Frank?" Mrs. Kirby called. "Who are you talking to?"

I groaned.

"It's okay, Nancy," he called. "We've got company. Kid says he knows you."

He tugged on my hood, propelling me toward the cottage and up the steps. For weeks, I'd been observing those stairs. Now I was actually climbing them, trapped in a nightmare.

Mrs. Kirby stood at the door holding the kid, wrapped in a towel. Instinctively, she retreated as we entered the house. "Who is it, Frank?"

"It's me, Christopher," I blurted out, "from Save 'n' Rave."

The kid started wailing. "Hush, Ryan," she said. "Why, it's you, Christopher." She looked from me to her husband. "What are you doing with him, Frank?"

He loosened his grip on my hood. I took a deep breath. "I found him outside the house, a regular Peeping Tom."

"I'm not a Peeping Tom," I said, my voice hoarse. "I visit Granite Cove Beach all the time. I've been coming here for years."

He lowered his face until we were so close I smelled sausage on his breath. "Yeah, kid? Then why were you hiding outside our house, in the grass?"

I paused for a second and cleared my throat. "I was looking for sand lizards ... I study them." I said this so earnestly that even *I* believed it.

"Looking for lizards *at night*?"

I nodded. "They come out at night, you see, and lay their eggs in the sand on the edge of the dune." I pointed in that general direction.

Mrs. Kirby moved to place a hand on my shoulder. "Christopher is a hard-working young man. He's been helpful to me at the market. He carried Butchie's dog food to the car." Her voice broke a little at the mention of the old dog.

"I'm really sorry he's gone, Mrs. Kirby," I said, nodding sympathetically.

El Stubbo crossed hairy arms over his chest. "I still think we should call the cops." He studied me with narrowed eyes. At that moment, he was the scariest person I'd ever met. "Who's your old man? I'll call, have him come get you."

When I told him, he said, "Koski? You mean the hardware store Koski?"

I nodded. "My dad's abandoned us," I said, lowering my eyes. "He lives somewhere else, with another family." I looked pleadingly at each of them, including the kid, whose finger was up his nose. If I hadn't been so nervous, I'd have squeezed out a couple of tears.

He pointed to a phone on a table. "Call your mother, then. I'll talk to her."

I shook my head. "Mom's reading to blind patients at the hospital." I took a deep breath. "I have a biology project that's due tomorrow. She doesn't know I'm here searching for sand lizards. She'd get awfully mad if she knew I waited until the last minute. Anyway, my bike's down the road. I was just about to leave. Tonight's too cold for lizards."

El Stubbo put a protective arm around his wife and son. "Get going, kid," he said. "You're lucky I wasn't carrying a gun tonight. I don't like trespassers or snoops."

Mrs. Kirby pulled away. "Frank, that's enough. He's only a boy." She went to the door and held it open. "Be careful riding home, Christopher." She patted my shoulder as I went out.

I walked stiffly to the edge of the dune, feeling their eyes upon me. In no time I was over the side, rolling like a log until I reached the bottom. A moment later, I was on my feet, racing along the boardwalk. I felt as if I could go for miles. As I ran, I heard a roaring in my ears that wasn't the ocean.

Fortunately, Mom's car was gone when I got home. I flew up the stairs to my room. There I sat on the edge of my bed, looking out the window. The street light cast a dull glow on the overgrown lot across the road. When I was little, I kept the shade pulled so I didn't have to see it. The lot was spooky; I was sure monsters lived in the dense shrubbery. When I got older, I was convinced it was a place for UFO activity. I'd kneel at the window, waiting to see a glowing spaceship hovering over the stunted pines. I had it all planned—I would run out to greet the aliens, my arms held high over my head. I wouldn't resist when they took me.

Now I moved to lean my forehead against the window pane. Staring at the shadowy lot, I prayed the aliens would appear. I imagined Mom discovering my empty bed. The police would be called. The neighbors would organize a search. My parents would appear on TV, Mom crying, Dad grim, his arm around her. They'd publicly beg for my return.

Meanwhile, the news media, desperate for information, sought interviews with my teachers. Mr. Ryan would call me a "brilliant" writer, and "my finest student." Eventually, the *Enquirer* would uncover how, the afternoon of my abduction, I was banished from the Murrays' house: "Abducted Boy Turned Away Like Stray Dog." The enraged community would retaliate. They'd throw stones at the Murrays' windows and drive over their lawn. Evan's sister, Katrina, would be bullied until she dropped out of school. Mr. Murray would lose his job, and Mrs. Murray would resign as president of the PTO following a nervous breakdown.

A similar fate awaited Mr. Kirby. A tearful Mrs. Kirby, interviewed on TV, would claim, "Christopher only wanted to study sand lizards outside our cottage." When El Stubbo got death threats, she'd leave him, taking the kid.

Suddenly exhausted, I moved from the window and crawled into bed fully clothed, including my sneakers. After putting the pillow over my head, I squashed it down, trying to force the evening's events from my brain.

It was the worst night of my life.

TEN

The next afternoon, I was slapping stickers on grapefruit. When I glanced up, I saw my mom rushing through the automatic doors. Actually, it's impossible to rush through the doors because they're so slow. Mom, however, burst into the store, coming to a halt in front of Mr. Zagrobski.

I automatically ducked my head when he pointed in my direction. Mom's face was blotchy, like she'd been crying. I continued applying stickers as she approached.

"Christopher, can we go someplace for coffee?"

"I don't drink coffee, Mom."

"Listen, we've got to talk. I don't want to do it here. My car's in the lot out back." She took a mirror from her bag and held it to her face. "Good God, I look like hell. I didn't even put mascara on. I just kicked off my slippers and came right over here."

I continued sticking stickers. "What's wrong?"

"Can you believe your father came to the door and

rang the bell? I'm working from home today, revising documents for Mr. Farley."

"What's wrong with Dad coming to the door?"

"That man has not stepped foot on my doorstep since the divorce. Imagine the scare he gave me." She whimpered and looked like she was going to cry again.

"Let's go outside to the car. I'll take my break now."

Mr. Zagrobski looked annoyed when I asked to take my break early. He made a big deal of looking at his watch until Mom told him, "It's a family emergency." He nodded glumly, giving the impression the store would close if I didn't get all the stickers on the grapefruit.

I led Mom to the back, where we used the employees' exit. Outside, it was one of those hot spring days that make you think summer's coming. People got excited about the heat. They removed their storm windows and put out the patio furniture. The next day it would snow, and they'd be back wearing parkas.

We walked to Mom's Subaru. I was the first to speak. "Thanks for telling my boss it's an emergency. What if he asks what it is?"

"It *is* an emergency, Christopher. What happened to you is what any parent would call an emergency."

I was so sure she didn't know about last night at the Kirbys that I asked, "And what is that?"

"You're turning into a problem child!"

She burst into tears and slid into the driver's seat. I opened the passenger door and got in, hoping no one saw us. Inside, the car was warm. Mom put a key in the ignition and rolled down the windows. Bad timing: a big, stupid, SUV with a half-dozen kids pulled into the space next to us. They all noisily leaped out. When they saw Mom crying, they stopped to stare, like we were monkeys at the zoo. I pressed the button to put my window up but the key was no longer in the ignition. If I'd had a paper bag I'd have put it over my head; anything to hide from the staring, snot-nosed kids. Finally, their mother got out and shooed them into the store.

I opened the glove compartment and pulled out a wad of Burger King napkins, handing them to her. I asked, "So, what did Dad want?"

"He said he'll be awarded custody based on new information from a Mr. Crosby of Granite Cove Beach."

"Kirby."

"Kirby, right. He said the new information will convince the judge you're not being supervised properly." She blew her nose and continued, "Finally, the court will award custody to your father." She scared me by pounding the dashboard with her fist. "I should have walked out at our reception. What was I doing with a man who wouldn't dance at his own wedding?"

I was happy to turn the conversation away from me. "Why didn't he dance?"

"Because he's uptight. He was born uptight. For that special day he wouldn't dance, even after four rum and cokes."

"Wow."

"I knew your father didn't like to dance. However, I never thought he'd refuse on his wedding day." She turned to look at me. "Remember, I was chosen 'Best Dancer' in my senior year. Those awards aren't given to just anyone. You have to earn them. Everyone knew I loved to dance and was good at it." She smiled and gazed out the window. "The cheerleading coach said I should continue, professionally." Then she remembered where she was and why. "So why did I marry someone who couldn't—and wouldn't—dance?"

I thought about it for a moment. "Dad was probably nervous, all those people looking at him."

She shook her head slowly. "I was forced to dance with my dad and my friends' husbands. Even Pastor Chitwick danced with me."

"What was Dad doing while you were dancing?"

"At one point I found him drawing a diagram, showing some guys the new addition to the store."

"What about Gramps? Did he dance at the wedding?"

She let out her breath. "My in-laws? They went to the church but never showed up at the reception. Something about your grandmother's gall stones. Truth was they never approved of me."

I couldn't think of anything to say because she was right. I glanced at the dashboard clock. "I'd better get back before Mr. Zagrobski has a cow."

"Okay, honey." She put a hand on my shoulder. "First, tell me why you were at Granite Cove Beach last night. You were supposed to be at home. You weren't really staring into the Kirbys' windows, were you?" She winced, like it hurt to ask.

My face got hot. "'Course not. What do you think I am, some kinda perv?"

"No, I don't, Christopher. In fact, I didn't believe what your father told me. He'll exaggerate about anything to win his case."

"I was looking for sand lizards, for my biology class project. I told Mr. Kirby, and he seemed to accept it. I don't know why he contacted Dad."

She attempted a smile. "I figured it was something like that. Yet it won't look good to Dr. Hutch, the therapist. Make sure you explain it when you see her tomorrow. Why didn't you tell me you were going over there?"

"Would you have let me go?"

"No, I suppose not." She took my hand. "Don't do it again. Do you want to scare me to death?"

I pulled away. "Mom, I've gotta get back."

"Okay. We'll talk more at home. By the way, is Mr. Zagrobski married?"

"Uh-huh, with four kids."

"Good Lord. What I need is someone mature ... and cultured."

SHARON LOVE COOK

"What about your boss, Mr. Farley?"

"He's too mature. He'll be eighty next winter. Besides, he's got a wife in a nursing home." She leaned over to kiss my cheek. "Be strong for me, Christopher. We'll get through this together." I nodded and opened the door. Before I could hop out, she said, "Guess what?"

"What?"

"During this crisis, from the time your father appeared at my door to drop his bombshell, I've only had two cigarettes. Normally I'd have finished the whole pack."

"That's really good, Mom."

I watched her drive away. I was glad she'd chilled, yet at the same time I felt sick. If anyone had looked at me, they'd have seen a black cloud hovering over me. The cloud was named "dread," and it had Mr. Kirby's face. I remembered, again, that face in the moonlight, the huge nostrils, the sausage-breath in my face. How could I go back to Granite Cove Beach after what happened? And now, what if the judge thinks I'm a Peeping Tom?

Back inside the store, I had an answer ready in case Mr. Zagrobski asked about the family emergency. "Gallstones," I was going to say. "My grandmother's." Instead, he must have forgotten. He told me to unpack and shelve, according to size, two cartons of adult diapers that had come in earlier.

As I unloaded them, I thought about grown-ups

and their weird world. In four years I'd be eighteen, an adult. I hoped I didn't act like my parents. Dad was always talking about the hardware store, like there was nothing beyond the world of extension cords and custom shades. Mom was always mentioning her high school days, like she was still living them.

I wished, when I got old, to be like Mr. Ryan. He was proof you didn't have to grow up and be lame.

The following afternoon, I had my first session with Dr. Hutch. I came home directly after school, as promised. Mom was at the counter, tending to a naked chicken sitting in a pan. She wore a pair of new oven mitts so stiff they didn't bend when she attempted to lift the pan. She pulled them off and threw them on the counter.

"What's up?" I asked, entering the kitchen.

"Honey, do you know how long I should cook this?" She studied an open cookbook sitting nearby. "This damn book has a hundred recipes for chicken but doesn't say how long to cook one."

I shrugged. "Why don't you call Grams? She's always cooking chicken."

"Oh, right, and give her something to hoot about."

"You mean something to cluck about."

Mom didn't recognize my remark as a joke. She was in a world of her own, acting the role of "wholesome mother." She turned on the oven. "I'll put it in for an hour. I don't have time to fool with it now. Dr. Hutch will be here any minute."

"Why don't you cook it after she goes?"

"Because I think it smells nice, a chicken in the oven."

I looked around the kitchen. She had set the stage. From the frilly apron that looked like something out of *Little House on the Prairie*, to the gleaming toaster, Mom had worked hard to impress the therapist.

A loud knock on the door made us jump. She clutched my arm; her hands were cold. "It's her. Now, remember: if she asks about your goals, say you want to become an Eagle Scout."

"But I'm not even a Boy Scout."

"She doesn't know that. Besides, you say you 'want to' become one. It doesn't mean you're actually working on it."

I hung back as Mom went to the door. Soon a tall, thin woman with gray hair pulled back in a knot entered the foyer. She wore a boxy-looking suit the color of corn flakes and carried a black brief case. She peered at Mom over heavy-looking eyeglasses, muttering a greeting. Mom ushered her in and introduced me. We shook hands.

"Lovely to meet you, Christopher," she said. Beady eyes behind the thick lenses studied me.

"Me too," I said, although it wasn't lovely. In fact, it was bad, almost as bad as the time I'd had an infected toenail removed.

Dr. Hutch dropped my hand and looked around. "Is there a place where Christopher and I could talk without being disturbed?"

"Why don't you go into the study?" Mom said.

"Fine," the therapist said.

Together we followed Mom down the hallway. Her frilly apron was tied in a big bow, like Alice in Wonderland. The study, like the kitchen, was neat and clean. The ashtrays were gone and the shag rug had been vacuumed. Mom patted the old sofa. "Sit here, Dr.Hutch. I'm making a slipcover for this, but it's still comfortable."

"My, aren't you talented," Dr. Hutch said.

I almost laughed aloud at Mom's remark. She couldn't sew a button if her life depended on it. Dr. Hutch glanced around the room, nodding. "I think this will be fine. Thank you, Mrs. Koski."

After Mom left, closing the door behind her, Dr. Hutch set her briefcase on the end of the sofa. I sat on the opposite end. "Hmm, family photos," she said, and moved to the mantel over the fireplace. She silently examined the row of pictures Mom had set out. Earlier, she'd removed the photo of herself and Doreen in Florida. They wore bikinis and held drinks in hollowed-out pineapples. It's really heinous.

The room, with the door closed, was warm, like a cocoon. As Dr. Hutch studied the photos, I closed my eyes. My mind drifted to an entirely different scenario:

Dr. Hutch, with her back to me, pulls the pins from her hair and shakes it out. It's not gray; it's thick and dark. She turns to me and whips off her eyeglasses. At the same time, her suit jacket opens, revealing a low-cut tank-top.

My eyes pop. "Mrs. Kirby, it's you!"

She puts a finger to her lips. "Shh. That's right, Christopher. Disguising myself as Dr. Hutch was the only way I could get to you." She pulls me to my feet. "Tell me, angel, who do you want to live with? Your mother or your father?"

She stands close, her hands on my shoulders. I raise my eyes to look into hers. "I don't want to live with either of them. I want to live with you."

"I thought you'd say that. Quick, let's sneak out the front door. My car's outside."

"Christopher?"

I opened my eyes to see Dr. Hutch staring down at me. "Oh, sorry. I was meditating."

She lowered herself onto the sofa. "I thought you'd fallen asleep. What time do you go to bed?"

"Right after my homework ... pretty early."

"No TV at night?"

"Not till my homework's done. My mom checks it. Then she lets me watch something educational on PBS."

She stared at me. "Is that so?"

"Uh-huh. On weekends, I can watch for an hour."

I didn't know if Dr. Hutch, with her expressionless face, believed me. She bent and opened her briefcase, taking out a large notebook. "I'm going to ask you a few informal questions. This is not a test. These are questions that will help me get an idea of your likes and dislikes. How does that sound?" She stared at me. Her eyes behind the thick, murky lenses looked like olives in a jar.

I nodded, sensing a trap. "Sounds good."

She asked me basic stuff, like who was my best friend, my favorite sport, and other nonthreatening questions. After that was out of the way, she said, "Let's say you and best friend Evan are spending time together. What is the most enjoyable activity you could share?" She leaned toward me and lowered her voice. "Just you two, with no one watching."

I sat back against the sofa, feeling a little stunned. Her question was obviously a trap. Not only that, it sounded like Dr. Hutch was hinting about our favorite game, Phone Freaks. For a second I wondered if she'd somehow found out about Chester Dolby, the old guy we'd pranked. Maybe Evan, the turd, had told his mom and Mrs. Murray had reported me. One thing I knew—I wouldn't let down my guard with Dr. Hutch around.

"Okay," I said, leaning forward. "What we'd do is grab a couple of trash bags. Then we'd go to Kwik Pix. It's a convenience store next to where the school bus lets the kids off. As a result, there's lots of crap—I mean, trash—on the ground. A real eyesore. Evan and I would pick it up."

She stared at me for a long moment. "That would be a 'fun' activity?"

"Well, maybe not fun, but we'd get a lot of satisfaction from doing it. That area is a mess. Kids leave the store, they toss candy wrappers and cans on the ground. The store owner doesn't care. He never cleans it up."

"I see," she said. "And why would you mind anyone seeing you performing this activity?"

"Are you serious? The kids will think we're a couple of dorks."

"Dorks?"

"You know, nerds."

"Yes, I know what a nerd is."

Now she narrowed her eyes and watched me, saying nothing. I looked away. Maybe it was an interrogation trick to make me nervous so I'd admit I was lying. Had I gone too far with the goody image? I added, "And after we're through picking up the trash, we'd buy the biggest Slurpees and a ton of pumpkin fudge." After a pause, I said, "Maybe a few Ring Dings."

"Does your mother allow you sweets?"

"No, I have to sneak them." I glanced at her. "You won't tell, will you?"

"Anything you tell me is confidential, Christopher."

"That's one of the reasons I don't want to live at

my grandparents'. It's so far away, I'd never be able to see Evan. He's one of the smartest kids in school." Which wasn't a lie. "My grades are better since he's been tutoring me." A lie. "And you know what?"

"What's that?"

"This summer we plan to go to the senior center downtown and teach the old folks how to use computers. Evan's already called about it."

"Is that so?" I could tell she approved, the way she smiled at me. I made a mental note to tell Evan to call the senior center and propose such a project. By the time summer arrived, they'd have forgotten about it. Now she asked, "Couldn't someone at your grandparents' house drive you to Evan's?"

I shook my head. "My grandfather's too old, and he's only got one good arm. My grandmother doesn't have a driver's license." I held up three fingers. "She tried three times to get it."

"Oh, my. So you're saying the location of your grandparents' house would affect you negatively?"

I sighed. "Not only the location, the atmosphere. It's creepy. At night wild animals roam around. You can't sleep with coyotes howling all night." I'd decided not to mention the one-hundred-year-old toilet seat and no cable. I didn't want to lay it on too heavy.

"I imagine that would be worrisome," she said, scribbling in her notebook.

"Plus, I'd have to give up my job at Save 'n' Rave.

Their house would be too far to ride my bike." I stared down at my hands. "I'd hate to lose my job. I'm saving to go to a young writers' conference next summer. My English teacher, Mr. Ryan, says I have talent."

"I think that's quite admirable," she said, smiling for the second time.

"Thanks," I said. "I mean, thank you, Dr. Hutch."

ELEVEN

I was in Mr. Fontaine's computer class when the principal's secretary entered the room and handed him a note. He read it and said, "Christopher Koski, a message for you."

I got up, feeling my stomach drop to my knees. Had Mr. Kirby, the slimy toad, called the police? Maybe the cops were waiting for me in the principal's office.

I took the note from Mr. Fontaine and shoved it in my pocket. When I returned to my desk, Evan nudged me. "What's up?" It's the first thing he'd said to me since class started. We'd been avoiding each other, which is hard when you're sharing a desk.

I shrugged, took the note from my pocket and read: *Christopher, your father is picking you up after school today.*

Evan nudged me again. "What's it say?"

"My dad and I are going for pizza after school."

I'd never tell the nosy bugger the truth. Not after

the way the Murrays treated me, like a dog. No, it was worse—like a dog with rabies. Yet I wished Dad and I *were* going for pizza. Instead, we were headed for the Good Shepherd Academy for an interview.

Sherrie had set up an appointment with the headmaster. At first, I told Dad to forget it—I wasn't attending a Jesus school with a bunch of freaks. Dad, as always, didn't hear this. According to him, I don't know my own mind; he does.

Sometimes I wished I could cram a big 747 airplane with all the nosy, meddling people in my life. I'd send it to a remote island in the South Pacific, with no return flight. By the time they found their way back, I'd be an adult. They couldn't boss me around anymore.

After the last bell, I went outside and found Dad's station wagon idling in the parking lot. I got into the front seat, tossing my backpack onto the floor mat. "Hi," I said.

"Got a comb on you?" he asked, looking me over critically.

"Don't worry, Dad. Your hair looks fine."

Not too long ago we'd have laughed at that. Now it seems like I'm walking on eggshells around him. He's always brooding about the custody battle, the lawyer's fees. At the same time, it's hard to feel sympathy. He created the problem. Why can't he just chill out, let me be me?

"Button the top of your shirt," he said. "You want to look presentable for Dr. Higganbottam."

"Who's that?" I asked, although I knew.

"He's the headmaster of Good Shepherd Academy."

"He's a doctor?"

"He has a doctorate, an advanced degree. Sherrie says he's a peach."

"A peach," I repeated. Did that mean he was round and fuzzy? I sighed.

The Good Shepherd Academy occupied a building that was once the local post office distribution center. The school had painted the original cinderblock facade a tangerine color. We parked in the visitors' lot. Dad locked the car and together we approached the entrance, neither of us speaking. "Will Sherrie be here?" I finally asked.

"No, she's taking your grandfather to his gastroenterologist."

If I hadn't felt like a lamb heading to the slaughter, I'd have asked what's a gastroenterologist. Thus it was fitting that an arched sign over the school entrance read: "A good shepherd guides his flock" (to the slaughter). Inside, the cinderblocks, painted yellow, were hung with homemade illustrated posters. One stated: "A Quitter Never Wins and a Winner Never Quits." Another claimed: "Believe, and Anything is Possible!"

After Dad gave our names at a small office, we

stood in the foyer. Dad, studying the posters, looked pleased. "Good Shepherd students get accepted to top colleges. Did you know that?"

He'd mentioned it more than once. "How thrilling for them," I muttered. When he scowled, I added, "But it has nothing to do with me."

He clamped a hand on my shoulder. "I'm only asking that you put your best foot forward today." He tightened his grip. I nodded.

A buzzer sounded and seconds later the hallway was filled with students. They headed for the entrance in an orderly way, no pushing or shoving. It was a sharp contrast to the deafening stampede at my school. Looking at the well-behaved students, it was hard to believe they were in high school. They looked like normal kids, though one or two wore tie-dyed shirts. I studied them until the receptionist called out: "Dr. Higganbottam will see you."

Dad thanked her and led me down a cinderblock corridor; these blocks were painted blue. A large man standing at the end smiled and opened his arms. He wore a knitted vest, the kind Gramps wears, only this was stretched across a massive belly. His silver hair was thick and wavy. His wire-framed glasses glinted in the light. Give him a beard and he'd make an excellent Santa Claus.

"Mr. Koski, I'm delighted to meet you and Christopher." He grabbed our hands in his big paws. "Come in, my friends." He led us into an office that had a desk and four old-looking wooden chairs. An old-fashioned spinning wheel stood in a corner. Two windows looked out onto a field where, outside, a cow and some sheep grazed. Farther away stood a red wooden barn. It was like a picture in a calendar of Olde New England.

"Appledrop Farm," he said, noting my interest. "It's a popular co-op. They've been wonderful neighbors. We'll be sorry to leave."

"Sherrie mentioned you might be moving," Dad said. He lowered himself into the chair as if expecting it to collapse under him.

The headmaster lowered himself into a tufted leather chair. It made a farting noise when he sat. A plaque on his desk said: *Dr. Clayton M. Higganbottam*. He leaned back in his chair. "Basically, we've outgrown this building. I always knew it would be temporary, but I didn't think we'd leave this soon. We need to make room for incoming students." He turned to me and said loudly, as if I were deaf, "How do you feel about attending Good Shepherd, Christopher?"

I nearly jumped in my seat. Although I had prepared a response, I hadn't expected the moment to come so soon. After all, we hadn't even had a tour of the school. I looked at Dr. Higganbottam and took a deep breath. "I don't think I qualify, sir."

He raised his bushy white eyebrows. "And why is that?"

I felt Dad's eyes boring into me when I said, "Because I don't believe in God."

"Christopher!" Dad practically leaped from his chair. "What kind of foolish talk is that?" He addressed the headmaster. "Pay no attention to that remark, Dr. Higganbottam. His mother, a lapsed Catholic, puts ideas in Christopher's head."

The headmaster waved away Dad's response. "Please, Mr. Koski, I have no problem with Christopher's answer. In fact, I admire his gumption. That's a quality we value here at Good Shepherd—independent thinking."

I squirmed in my chair as he beamed at me. My remark had been carefully considered, and it wasn't entirely true. Although I *am* a believer, my God isn't the same as my dad's. His is a man in a long white nightgown. Mine is Master of the Universe or, like the Native Americans' deity, the Great Spirit.

Dr. Higganbottam continued: "We don't require our students to be Christians, although many are. What we value is integrity and honesty. It appears that Christopher's got plenty of both."

Inside, I groaned. Dr. Higganbottam liked me.

We drove home in silence. That was okay with me. At least Dad wasn't mad. I hadn't—unfortunately—blown my chances at Good Shepherd. When we stopped in front of the house, he sat there, looking around at the yard. "Tell your mother not to cut the lilacs back until they finish blooming."

"Okay." I paused. "Dad, are you taking me out on my birthday this year?"

"I'd like to Christopher, but we're swamped at the store. You know how Sherrie talked me into stocking more garden supplies?"

I nodded. He'd said something, but I hadn't paid much attention. Sherrie was always running the show, at my grandparents' house and at the store.

"It's taken off in a big way. I may have to hire a new clerk for the summer." He looked at me. "Anytime you get tired of working at Save 'n' Rave, let me know. I could use a good stockboy."

It was Dad's way of making up to me for missing my birthday. "If you're not going to take me out this year, I'm thinking of having some friends over for pizza and cake."

"Really? Where?"

I rolled my eyes. "At home, of course."

"With your mother chaperoning?"

I shrugged. "Yeah. Who else?"

He frowned. "Your friends' parents won't approve if your mother is the chaperone. She's liable to have a couple of drinks and fall asleep. With no supervision, kids can get into trouble."

"Dad, it's just pizza and birthday cake."

"There's the liability issue to consider. My lawyer says a host, if proven negligent in a lawsuit, could lose his house."

"Dad, these are my friends. They're not going to trash the house."

"I'll tell you what. How 'bout if Sherrie plans a party at your grandparents'. She'll make snacks and organize fun games. How does that sound?"

To be honest, it sounded painful. I tried to imagine Alyssa Putnam's reaction to my grandparents' reindeer head in the living room. What would she think about the old-fashioned tub with its claw feet, or the ancient wooden toilet seat? How would Shawna Curran react to Gramps's dead arm with the gnarled, claw-like fingers? If that wasn't bad enough, imagine their reaction to the wild animals screeching in the dark.

"Let me think about it, Dad."

I got out of the car. Before going inside, I turned and waved. Inside, I went directly to my room: finally, *freedom*.

TWELVE

Friday afternoon we took the bus into Boston for the student reading. I sat with Evan, as we'd planned earlier. Although things were still awkward between us, I didn't dwell on it. I was too distracted, thinking about the reading. Last night, I'd had trouble sleeping, imagining the auditorium filled with strangers. Kids can be tough. What if they heckled me? Richie, sitting with Vinnie, must have read my mind. He turned and said, "Chris, are you afraid you'll pee your pants at the podium?"

"I hadn't thought about it," I lied.

Shawna Curran, another reader, overheard the question. "I'm not scared to read," she said. "I have a message people need to hear."

"I'd be wicked nervous." Richie stuffed a handful of potato chips into his mouth.

Vinnie gave him a sour look. "Blubber boy, you'd never get to read. The minute you walked onto the stage, it'd collapse under your weight." He threw his head back and laughed at his joke.

"Cut it out, Vinnie. That's bullying," Alyssa Putnam jabbed his shoulder with her index finger.

Vinnie's laughter was cut short when Ms. Carbone came down the aisle. He gaped at the teacher who wore tight pink pants and a short white jacket. Shawna nudged Alyssa. "Ms. Carbone's showing off her spray-on slacks." They watched her move to the front of the bus where she had a brief conversation with the driver. When she returned to her seat, Shawna said, "I'll bet that was totally unnecessary. She probably asked, 'How's the driving, honey?' just so she could bend over and show her butt." "Yeah," Vinnie said. "I wish she'd do it again."

"She's hoping Mr. Ryan's watching," Alyssa said.

"Hey, girls," Vinnie said, looking around. "Do you like poetry?"

"I love poetry," Shawna said. "I'm going to be a poet when I grow up."

"Me, too," Alyssa said. "Like Emily Dickinson. And when I die, my fans will make a pilgrimage to Granite Cove to visit my house."

"Then listen to this poem," Vinnie said. "I just made it up about Ms. Carbone." He waited until he had their attention and said, "Mr. Ryan will leave her cryin,' but ole Vinnie will make her whinny."

Richie laughed, spraying potato chips on the girls' hair. They shrieked in protest, shaking their heads. Vinnie grabbed the bag from Richie and threw it out the bus window. "Can't you go anywhere without stuffing your pie hole?"

"I have to eat or my blood sugar drops," Richie said, checking his pockets for candy. "Hey, Vinnie, are you going to Peking Palace with me after the reading?"

"Blubber boy, I got my night planned. It don't include eating lo mein with losers."

"What're you gonna do?"

"I'm going to a party at my cousin's in East Boston."

"Are you gonna ask the bus driver to drop you off?"

Vinnie slapped his forehead. "Is your whole family pathetic like you? Do you really think I'd ask the bus driver to do that?"

"You'd better not let Mr. Ryan know you're not taking the bus home," Richie said.

"Big deal. I'm seventeen. I don't need permission like you babies."

Inside, the Addison College theater rang with students' voices despite teachers' efforts to quiet them. We walked in through the swinging doors at the rear and looked around in awe. The theater was huge, its audience filling row upon row. According to Mr. Ryan, ten Boston-area high schools were represented.

As he led us down the center aisle to our reserved section, I searched the crowd for my parents. Dad was coming alone, while Mom was driving in with Doreen.

Once seated, I gazed at the sea of students, a feeling of dread building inside me. I wished I could have Shawna's attitude; she felt her essay was a gift to mankind. I took a deep breath—my chest was tight—and let it out shakily.

"Koz, how do you feel?" Evan asked, nudging me.

Like I'm hollow, I wanted to confess. And I would have, but not to the "new" Evan, who appeared to be enjoying my stage fright, judging by the smirk on his face. Instead, I shrugged and said, "I'll get through it."

"Just remember," he said, "outside of our class, no one knows you here. So if you screw up, it's no big deal."

"I'm glad I have your permission," I told him.

Mr. Ryan appeared at the end of our row and motioned to Shawna and me. When I stood, I almost toppled, my body was so stiff. As I moved down the aisle, Evan called, "Remember, it's okay to screw up." His tone had an edge. It made me aware that Evan Murray was jealous—*of me!* Writing is the only subject in which he doesn't excel. *He wants me to fail,* I thought. The realization made me want to succeed.

I continued to the end of the row, passing in front of each seated student. Richie, unfortunately, was a tight fit. He had to stand and press himself against the (folded) seat, one hand clutching a bag of M&Ms. "You're gonna be awesome, Chris," he told me.

"Yeah," Vinnie said. "Wake me when it's his turn, will ya, blubber boy?"

I smiled. "Thanks, guys."

Shawna, after a brief conversation with Mr. Ryan, skipped down the aisle and mounted the steps at the end of the stage. Mr. Ryan faced me, his back to the audience. "Chris, if you have second thoughts, I'll read your essay for you."

I looked at the brightly-lit stage and swallowed. "Thanks, Mr. Ryan. I've come all this way; I should read it myself."

"I was hoping you'd say that. A writer knows his work better than anyone." He pointed to the stairs. "Go on backstage with Shawna. I'll join you later."

As I walked up the steps, the house lights dimmed. At the same time, the stage lights got brighter. A spotlight illuminated a podium near the front. I patted my pocket for the twentieth time, making sure my essay was inside. After a quick search, I found an opening in the curtain and joined the readers backstage. The program started when a large man in a baggy suit approached the podium. He introduced the founder, a white-haired lady named Eleanor Bickerton. She hobbled across the stage, her cane loudly thumping the floor. In a gravely voice, she welcomed everyone to the "fifteenth annual Boston-Area Student Reading," calling it a prestigious event. "I've known students who've appeared here go on to become acclaimed writers." She mentioned a few names, none I recognized. That wasn't surprising. I like sci-fi and horror, something Mrs. Bickerton probably doesn't read. "We'll go in alphabetical order, starting with Allston High School. Each school's teacher will introduce the reader and the essay title." She peered out at the audience, shielding her eyes from the glare. "Please be respectful while students are reading."

The large man who'd introduced her crossed the stage. He leaned into the microphone and thanked Mrs. Bickerton. "The program will now begin." With that, he led her off the stage. At the same time, Allston's English teacher climbed the steps to the stage to introduce the first reader.

Shawna appeared next to me and squeezed my hand. "We won't have to wait long," she whispered. "Do you mind if I go first?" I shook my head. "I can't wait," she said. "My aunt's going to film my reading."

"They said not to take photos," I said.

"Oh, that's for people who stand up, blocking everyone's view."

I nodded, not wanting to talk about the readings. I had a sick feeling in my stomach. It was like when I visited Hysteria Haunted Farm, where zombies hiding in the corn fields jump out at you. I was ten years old and pretending to be brave. Now I took a box of cherry cough drops from my pocket. They always made me feel better ... most of the time.

I left Shawna and moved backstage. There, heavy curtains served as partitions, creating a sense of privacy. A few students had paired off to practice reading their essays. I found a plastic milk crate and sat. In the dim light I closed my eyes and listened to the voices swirling around me. It was calming, and took my mind off my upcoming turn at the podium. Time passed until I heard Mr. Ryan's amplified voice saying Shawna's name. My heart lurched. For a while I sat frozen. Finally, I forced myself to rise and move to the front.

Shawna stood at the podium. The spotlight created a halo around her blond hair. Speaking too fast, she'd already reached the end of her essay: "And when I become a supermodel, I won't be the celebrity-type we're so familiar with. Instead, I'll use my popularity to raise money and draw attention to refugees and AIDS sufferers. I'll visit homeless shelters and let them know they're not alone, that *someone* cares. I'll give them something more meaningful than money. I'll give them hope."

The audience's response, which included a few whistles, was loud. Shawna clutched her essay to her chest, basking in the applause. When Mr. Ryan approached the podium, she reluctantly moved away. The audience quieted and he said, "Next is Christopher Koski, a freshman at Granite Cove High. He'll read his essay titled, 'Christmas Eve and Long Ago.'"

I moved across the stage on wooden legs. Mr. Ryan, in passing, gave me a thumbs-up. I tried to smile but my face was frozen. At the podium, I looked into the light's glare. Its brightness prevented me from seeing the audience. All I could make out were shadowy forms in the first row. Everyone else was a blur. For the moment, I could pretend there was no one seated beyond the first row. I took a breath and began:

"Sometimes in life it's not the big things that stay in your mind—the family vacation or the bike you got for your birthday. Those things are nice, but over time their appeal fades. Before long, you've forgotten which birthday it was when you got the bike, and where you'd gone on that vacation. Lately I've learned it's the small things, like time spent with family, that leave an impression on your mind."

I stared down at my speech, realizing that I knew it by heart. I didn't have to read it. I looked out at the audience located somewhere beyond the lights. A cocoon of warmth surrounded me. My time at the podium would be brief. I wouldn't rush through my story. I continued until I reached the end, where my family leaves the church following Midnight Mass: "When we filed out of church, we discovered it had snowed while we were inside. It covered the concrete steps of the church and the cars lining the street. As we walked home, we saw the familiar landscape transformed. Snow encased the neighbors' trees, strung with Christmas lights. Covered in a blanket of white, they glowed from within.

"The only sound was the snow crunching under our feet. Otherwise, the world had gone silent. I felt like we were the only people on Earth, and I wished the night would never end. Although I can't recall the presents I got that year, I remember my family's walk home on Christmas Eve. It's a memory I'll keep for the rest of my life."

There was a pause followed by applause and cheering. Mr. Ryan appeared at my side. He lowered his head to say, "Terrific, Chris."

I smiled up at him. "I stopped being nervous."

"Good for you. Go and join the others backstage."

Mr. Ryan then announced the next readers, from Hull High School. He waited for their teacher to take the podium. But instead of going backstage, he went down the side steps. Ms. Carbone waited at the bottom.

Backstage, Shawna said, "Christopher Koski, you made me cry." She blotted her eyes with a tissue.

"I did? That's great. I mean, I'm sorry, but at the same time—"

She laughed. "Don't explain, dummy. But seriously, you were awesome."

My face burned. "You were pretty awesome yourself." I pulled out the box of cough drops. "Want one?"

"Sure." She reached inside. "Now I've got to join Alyssa. I said I'd sit with her after I read."

"Mr. Ryan wants us to stay back here until it's finished."

"Oh, really? Did you see him scooting off to join Pink Pants?"

I shrugged. "Yeah, but he's the teacher. They make the rules."

She patted my cheek. "We're in high school, Christopher, not grade school."

With that she slipped away. I didn't mind. I wanted to think about my recent experience. Something had happened to me onstage. I went out there like a hollow shell, but then at some point I'd felt a connection with the audience. I'd known I would be okay.

I returned to the milk crate behind the curtain and sat. The kids who hadn't gone on yet were practicing in pairs. I listened, hearing the nervousness in their voices. I wanted to tell them to not be afraid, that it wasn't bad. In fact, it was awesome.

"Everyone onstage!"

I jumped up and joined the others. The student readers and teachers stood in a semi-circle, their arms around each other. Squashed together, we faced the audience. They gave us a standing ovation. I looked out at the crowd, hoping my parents could see me. Someone brought out a bouquet of roses for Mrs. Bickerton. She was whisked onto the stage in a wheelchair. We all stood around her, clapping. I wished it would go on and on, but soon the curtain came down.

I approached Mr. Ryan. "Is it okay if I say hi to my parents?"

"Do you know where they're sitting?"

"I think so."

"Okay." He glanced at his watch. "Be back at the bus in twenty minutes sharp."

I raced down the steps and was immediately caught up in the mob heading for the door. I wormed my way through the crowd, jumping up and down in an attempt to see over their heads. I spotted my dad near the back of the theater. I'd never reach him in time, surrounded by the slowly exiting mass. I climbed onto the armrest of a nearby seat. Jumping from one chair to another like a mountain goat, I reached him.

He spotted me and frowned. "That's not very smart, son. People know who you are."

I jumped down to stand next to him. "Sorry, Dad, but it looked like you were leaving. I wanted to ask what you thought about my reading."

"It was very good. I couldn't help thinking that, if you put the same effort into math as you do writing, your grades would improve."

"Yeah … maybe." I looked around. "Is Mom still here?"

He struggled into his jacket. "I don't know. She probably left after you finished. I'll bet she and

Doreen stop for a drink on Route One."

I nodded. "Well, I gotta get back to the bus. I just wanted to say hi."

He pulled a long envelope from his pocket. "I waited to give you this personally."

"What is it?"

"Your birthday money. I don't want to send it in the mail."

I took the sealed envelope. "Thanks, Dad."

"You might want to open an account at Granite Cove Savings Bank."

I folded the envelope and put it in my pocket. "I wonder why Mom didn't stay."

"She left in a huff. You know how she can't tolerate bad news."

"Why? What'd you say to her?"

"I told her that my lawyer is filing what's called an Emergency Petition of Guardianship. It means you could be moving in with me as early as Monday."

"Dad, can you listen to me just once?" My voice must have been loud because people in the aisle stared.

He held up his hands, palms out. "At fourteen, you're not expected to understand. In the past month, you've come to the attention of the police. It would have been twice had Mr. Kirby contacted them following your last episode. Instead, he came to me because he's concerned, and so am I. With Mr. Kirby's written testimony, my lawyer says the court will approve the order. All I wanted to do was give your mother a heads-up. I can't help it if she won't face reality."

I wanted to explain about being at Granite Cove Beach. At the same time, I was afraid my voice would shake. "Thanks for coming," I told him. "I've got to find my teacher now."

"Son, wait–"

I moved to the aisle. Keeping my head down, I wove my way through the crowd heading in the opposite direction. When I reached the stairs, I bounded up them to the darkened stage. I hoped Mr. Ryan was still around.

I located the opening in the billowy curtains and went through. In the dimness backstage, I heard sounds. I stopped and peered at a shadowy couple standing inside a partition, their arms around each other. I was slinking away when the woman said, "Uh-oh, we've got company." It was Ms. Carbone. She was with Mr. Ryan.

He quickly stepped away from her. "Chris, I thought you were on the bus."

"Ah, that's what I need to ask you about. My dad wants to take me out for a celebration dinner."

"We usually require such requests in advance." He paused. "But I saw the two of you together, so I'm sure it'll be fine." He took a step toward me. "You did a great job, Chris."

"Thanks. I've gotta go now."

I turned and quickly retraced my steps. The auditorium was mostly empty. A guy was vacuuming the rug that ran the length of the aisle. He didn't look up when I raced past, sprinting toward the swinging doors and out to the street.

THIRTEEN

I stood on Boylston Street and took the envelope from my pocket. Inside was a hundred dollar bill. With the birthday money, and what I had in my pocket, I could buy a bus ticket to New York City. Nobody could find me there.

I walked to the crossing and waited for the light to change. The traffic and street noise made my head spin like the Scrambler at the carnival. Did I really want to go to New York, a bigger and more crowded city? Unfortunately, I had no choice. If I wanted to stay hidden, that was where I should go. People in books and movies always go to New York City when they need to disappear.

I walked two blocks to the Econo Bus Terminal. I'd spotted it while en route to the theater, never imagining I'd later be visiting it. I went in a side door, my head down, my shoulders hunched. The terminal inside was also noisy. Sounds bounced off the high ceiling and echoed throughout the building.

I stood before a sign displaying a long list of bus routes. For a moment I toyed with the idea of going to Halifax, Nova Scotia, but I'd have to cross a border. Another basic rule of surveillance: Don't attract attention. Finally, I located the window selling tickets to New Haven, Hartford, and New York City.

I took a deep breath and approached the window. The woman behind the mesh screen didn't look up when I said, "I'd like a ticket to New York."

"New York's a big state. Where you wanna go, upstate? Long Island? Manhattan—"

"That's right, Manhattan. How much is that?"

She noticed me for the first time. "You traveling alone, honey? Where's a parent or guardian?"

I thought fast. "I'm—I'm with my grandmother. She's, ah, disabled and can't walk very good." I turned and scanned the room. An old lady in a black coat sat huddled on a long bench against the wall. I pointed at her. "That's Grams. She can't get up because of her withered leg. Do you want me to get her over here?" I jerked my thumb toward the entrance. "I saw a couple of wheelchairs by the door."

"Nah, you don't hafta do that. That's two tickets to Manhattan?"

"Just one, please. Grams has a ticket."

"That's thirty-five dollars. Bus leaves at eight-twenty at terminal seven."

"Okay." I placed the hundred-dollar bill into a

metal drawer that shot out. After putting my change away, I put the ticket into my backpack. I'd have to be careful if I wanted my money to last. Maybe I'd find a nice New York parish that'd let me sleep in a vacant pew in return for doing chores. I saw that in a TV movie once. The guy was an exiled prince who learned to live on his own. When the king called him back, he remained in hiding. I'd worry about lodgings when I arrived. Right now my mission was to get out of Boston.

In case the ticket seller was watching me, I headed across the room toward the old lady. As I slowly approached, I wondered what to say. After all, I was supposed to be her grandson. She sat hunched, eating shelled peanuts from a bag, her eyes darting around the room. "Excuse me, ma'am," I said loudly in case she was deaf, "can you tell me where you got those peanuts?" I pointed at the bag.

Looking alarmed, she shoved the bag into her pocket. A heavy man sitting next to her lowered his newspaper and glared. "Whatta ya want, kid?" When I didn't answer, he said, "Scram, get outta here." He turned to her. "It's okay, Mama." When she continued to watch me, her eyes wide with fright, he said something in a foreign language, patting her arm.

I found my voice and squeaked, "Thank you. Have a nice day."

I forced myself to walk away, a smile on my face in case the ticket lady was watching. I decided to escape to the men's room, but on the way my stomach growled. I hadn't had anything since a breakfast of Pop Tarts. If I didn't eat now, I'd never get a chance during the long bus ride.

I went outside the terminal and bought a Jumbo Jim's Dog from a vendor. When the guy—Jumbo Jim?—asked what I wanted on it, I pointed to every container: mustard, onions, relish, beans, sauerkraut. He gave me a dirty look but spooned on the condiments. I decided the people in Boston were a bunch of soreheads.

I took the messy but delicious dog inside, sitting on a bench against the wall. I looked at the passengers, those leaving and those arriving. I felt frightened but also excited to be one of them. I was claiming my independence, like the Boston Revolutionists. I wouldn't think about my destination or what I'd do upon arriving. I was living in the moment, or, as the Buddhists say, *Be here now.*

After finishing my hot dog, I went to a newsstand and bought a Snickers bar. Then I headed for the men's room. The smell of pine tree disinfectant was heavy, but the place looked clean. Best of all, I was alone. And because I wasn't about to pee in a public urinal, I went inside a stall and locked the door. As I was zipping up, the men's room door opened and someone entered. I stood frozen, waiting for whoever was there to finish their business and get the hell out. The voice startled me:

"Excuse me, young man. Are you in there?"

He sounded like one of those English actors on public TV.

"That's right," I said, looking under the stall door at the stranger's shiny black tie shoes. I'd seen similar shoes on attorney Spencer Thurston. However, I didn't think Mr. Thurston had followed me to the Econo Bus Terminal.

"You've left your pack out here. I'm afraid it'll be stolen."

I clamped a hand over my mouth. He was right! How stupid could I be? "Wait a minute," I said, opening the door an inch to peek out.

The man, his back to me, washed his hands at the sink. He wore a dark suit and, with his wavy silver hair, looked like the guy married to the Queen of England. He glanced at me in the mirror. "You're in a big city, son. Hooligans on every corner, waiting to snatch a bag or purse."

I edged out and grabbed my backpack from the floor. I wanted to check my money, but didn't want to insult the guy. After all, he wouldn't be warning me if he'd stolen it. "Thank you."

He wiped his hands on a paper towel, still smiling in the mirror. "My name is Graham, and I believe in looking out for young people."

"I'm Chris," I said, inching toward the exit. "Thanks again."

"Are you traveling alone, Chris?"

"Uh-huh, to New York City."

"Have you ever driven a Jaguar?"

"Uh, no, I don't have my license."

He laughed. "I'm sure you'd do better than the majority of Boston drivers. What do you think? Cash in your ticket. I'll take you right to your door."

"No, that's okay."

"Are you sure?"

He moved quickly for an old guy, suddenly closing the distance between us. I felt his hand on my waistband, pulling me toward him. I grabbed my backpack in both hands and slammed it into him. That sent him reeling backward against the sink, the back of his head hitting the mirror. I shot out the door and raced across the terminal to the main exit.

I didn't wait for the traffic light; I ran across the street, dodging cars. Drivers blasted their horns. A cop blew his whistle and yelled. I reached the opposite sidewalk and ran, my legs pumping, until finally I dropped to the curb. I threw my head back and gulped the cool night air.

After a while, I got to my feet. According to the clock outside the terminal, my bus would leave in forty minutes. As I walked back, I considered stopping to tell the cop about Graham in the men's room. Yet what was the point? I doubt the old perv would hang around the terminal. He'd probably moved to another place where he could prey on kids who were alone. I wondered if he really had a Jaguar.

I shook my head in disgust. Guys like that, looking distinguished, are the worst. They fool you into thinking they're normal.

Once inside the terminal, I scanned the room. No sign of Graham, nor did I expect to see any. I took a seat against the wall and pulled out my Snickers bar. Inside my backpack I found the copy of *Winesburg, Ohio*. The book was a loan from Mr. Ryan. It felt good holding it. I wondered if he was mad at me for lying to him. Of all the people I was leaving behind, Mr. Ryan was the one I'd miss the most.

I decided to call him from one of the old phones lining the wall. I heard you couldn't trace a call from a public phone if you didn't stay on the line. I'd leave him a message, apologizing for being a jerk. After inspecting the phones, I discovered they were mostly broken and beat up. Finally, I found one that worked. I opened the *Winesburg, Ohio* front cover where Mr. Ryan had written his name and phone number. My hands shook as I dropped in coins and punched in his number. On the first ring he said hello. "Mr. Ryan? This is Christopher Koski. I wanted to apologize for lying and to say goodbye." I stopped talking when I thought I'd start crying.

"Chris? Where are you calling from?"

"Boston. That's all I can say."

"Chris, tell me where you are."

It was noisy in the terminal. I covered my ear in order to hear him. "It's okay; I'm goin' on a trip. I'm gonna finish my manuscript, too, once I'm settled."

"Chris, tell me where you are. Everyone's worried."

"I'm in Boston, but I'm leaving soon. It's something I have to do."

"Chris—"

"Mr. Ryan, you're the best teacher I've ever had. I'm sorry I let you down."

"Please, Chris—"

A voice on the intercom announced bus number twenty-four boarding for Hartford, New Haven, and New York. "I gotta go now," I said, and hung up.

I blew my nose on a napkin. Then I carefully returned the paperback to my backpack and slung it over my shoulder. I crossed the room and joined a long line of people outside the doors of gate seven. The line moved slowly until finally we stood outside. A big silver bus parked at the curb hissed and spewed diesel exhaust. We waited under a plastic overhang whose lights were speckled with dead bugs. Beyond the line of buses, the darkening sky was slashed with purple streaks.

While I waited in the line, I watched my fellow passengers. I didn't want to share a seat with a solitary man. Before tonight, I'd have chosen someone like Graham—distinguished. It was clear I'd have to be constantly on my guard in New York. The city, I'd heard, was a mecca for freaks.

Two Indian ladies wearing shawls over their heads stepped up to board. At that moment, a commotion broke out inside the bus. The driver leaped from his seat and closed the door, barring our way. Everyone moved back, surprised. A man behind me said, "I think one of the passengers is sick." The woman with him muttered, "I *knew* we'd be late."

Through the windows, we watched people being herded to the back of the bus. The driver opened the door. He held up a hand, telling us, "Stay there." He climbed down the steps and rushed inside the terminal. The woman behind me said, "Says who?" She went up the steps and peeked inside.

Having gotten an eyeful, she joined us on the pavement. "Some guy's lying on the floor," she announced, "and someone's giving him CPR." She added, "Probably a heart attack."

We waited. The exhaust, hot and spewing into the air, made me feel sick. I took off my jacket and tied the sleeves around my waist. The driver returned, ignoring us as he boarded the bus. A few minutes later the sound of sirens filled the air. An ambulance pulled up behind the bus. Two EMTs leaped out, carrying a folded stretcher. They pushed past us and disappeared inside the bus. The nosy woman, now standing behind me, swore and tapped her watch.

A few minutes later the EMTs emerged, carrying a man. They maneuvered around before getting him down the steps. Even with the clear plastic mask covering his face, I recognized the person on the stretcher. It was the guy who'd yelled at me, telling me to scram. Following the stretcher was "Mama," the old lady in black, assisted by a passenger. We stood back, silent, and let them through.

After the ambulance roared away, their siren splitting the night air, the bus driver descended the stairs. He asked if we had any luggage to stow. An old lady with a tiny dog in a carrier said, "I'm not putting him in baggage. He sits with me."

"Everybody, get your tickets out," the driver said, bounding up the steps to take his seat. Once again, I followed the two ladies covered in shawls. I stood close behind them, hoping the driver would assume I was with them. They gripped the metal pole and pulled themselves up the steps. I stood on the bottom step, ticket in hand. Before I disappeared inside the bus, I turned for a final look. Who knew when I'd see Boston again?

My attention was caught by someone racing through the terminal doors and coming to a stop outside. It was Mr. Ryan.

FOURTEEN

I squeezed past the couple behind me and leaped to the pavement. I turned in the opposite direction, passing a row of steel buses. Their massive grills poured steam into the night air. I was headed for the parking lot beyond the terminal. There I could hide among the cars, or crawl under one. As I ran, I heard the pounding of feet behind me, but I didn't dare look back. I kept my head down, my legs pumping like crazy.

When I reached the parking lot, I discovered it was bordered by a chain-link fence. Before I was able to scale it, my legs went out from under me. I hit the pavement like a sack of wet sand. Mr. Ryan had tackled me! For a while, the two of us lay there, panting. My elbows and palms felt like I'd scorched them on a wood stove.

A shadow fell over me and someone said, "Hey, kid, you know this guy?"

I glanced up at a uniformed bus driver staring

down at me. I was too winded to answer. Mr. Ryan, sounding not winded at all, said, "Thanks. We're okay now."

"I wasn't asking you, buddy," the man said. "I was talking to the kid."

"Do you want to answer the man, Chris?" Mr. Ryan asked.

I pulled myself up to a sitting position. "Nah, it's okay. He's my teacher."

"If you say so." The bus driver took a few seconds to scowl at Mr. Ryan. "Some teacher," he said, before walking away, shaking his head.

"You made me miss my bus," I said. "I just lost thirty-five bucks."

"I'm sorry, Chris, but I had no choice." He got to his feet and held out a hand. "Come on. My car's in a tow zone. We'd better hurry."

I stumbled to my feet, ignoring his hand. My pants were torn and my knees stung. "I'm sorry you came all this way, Mr. Ryan, but I'm not going back home."

He pulled out a handkerchief and wiped his hands. "Running away from your problems is the easy way. It also allows you to punish those at home."

Although Mr. Ryan was a head taller than me, I stood up straight and looked him in the eye. "You don't know anything about me, Mr. Ryan. You don't even know what I'm running from. And who are you to give advice? I saw you backstage, kissing Ms.

Carbone. You pretend to be perfect, but you're as phony as everyone else."

Mr. Ryan paused, watching me. "I'm sorry you got the idea I'm perfect, Chris, because I'm far from perfect. I make mistakes like everyone else." He stuffed the handkerchief back into his pocket. "But how about you, up there on your perch, judging everyone. Isn't it lonesome, all alone up there?"

Although his words were cruel, his voice was kind, his expression patient. Something let go inside me, something I'd been holding back for a long time. Soon I was blubbering like a baby. After a moment, Mr. Ryan put his arms around me, patting my back. Eventually the crying gave way to hiccups. He handed me his handkerchief. I wiped my face.

We stood there, not speaking, until I said, "Where'd you learn to run like that?"

"Boston College. Track."

"You're good." I handed him his handkerchief.

"Thanks." He looked out at the street. "Let's get the car before the city tows me away." Together we walked through the terminal and out to the street.

During the ride home I told Mr. Ryan everything that'd happened to me that day. I told him about Graham in the men's room, and "Mama" with her peanuts, and her son who chased me away. I talked about later seeing the son on a stretcher, an oxygen mask strapped to his face.

"When you get home, write it all down," he said when I stopped.

We were going through Revere when he made a right into the parking lot of Kelly's Roast Beef. "I have to call your parents," he said. "They're waiting to hear from me." I stared glumly out the window, saying nothing. He added, "And I could use a roast beef sandwich with barbecue sauce. How about you?"

I realized I was starving. "Yeah, me too."

Inside, he told me to grab a booth while he searched for a pay phone. The waitress approached with a questioning look, asking if I was alone.

"I'm waiting for my .... . . friend," I told her. "Then we'll order."

"Okay, honey. Take a seat and I'll be back."

After several minutes, Mr. Ryan slid into the seat across from me. "They're very relieved," he said.

"They?"

"Your mom and dad. They're at your house now."

'They don't have to make a big deal about it," I said, sighing.

"Chris, it is a 'big deal,' especially to parents."

The waitress returned. We ordered Cokes, two jumbo roast beef sandwiches with barbecue sauce, and a side of French fries to share. When we were alone again, Mr. Ryan leaned back in his seat. "I don't want to be nosy, but do you mind telling me why you wanted to run away?"

I realized I had no excuses anymore. And somehow, Mr. Ryan made talking about my family seem natural. I told him about my dad's custody fight and his chances of winning.

"Courts don't usually take kids from their mothers unless there's a problem," he said. "Is she a good mother?"

I told him how Mom had been trying to quit smoking, and how she acted like a TV mom, especially in front of Dr. Hutch. "It's not Mom's fault," I said. "It's me, and what I did. I got caught spying on someone at night. Now everyone thinks there's no supervision at my house. The judge will hear about it and send me to live with my grandparents."

"Spying?"

Fortunately I didn't have to explain. The waitress brought our food to the table.

We were silent while we ate. It was the best roast beef sandwich I'd ever eaten. I laughed when Mr. Ryan dripped barbecue sauce down the front of his white shirt. He dipped his napkin in water and tried wiping it. That spread the stain more.

"Look at me," he said. "Torn pants, skinned knees, something on my shirt that looks like blood." He glanced at me. "And you're not much better. How are we going to see Vinnie, looking like this?"

I looked up. "Huh? Vinnie?"

"Yes, Vinnie, who is in Everett Hospital." He shook his head slowly. "I've had quite a night."

"What do you mean?"

He told me about getting my phone call and then

calling my parents. Immediately, he got a message from Everett Hospital. Vinnie, after leaving the party at his cousin's, had gotten jumped by some street guys. "Broken collarbone, broken rib. They're keeping him for observation in case of a concussion."

"Why did the hospital call *you*?" I asked.

"Apparently Vinnie lives with an aunt who's a truck driver, on the road a lot. He didn't know who else the hospital could notify. After that call, I updated the superintendent of schools."

"Gee, Mr. Ryan, I'm sorry. Did we get you in trouble?"

He placed his napkin on the table. "I imagine there'll be a hearing."

"Oh, no. Will you lose your job?"

"To be honest, this has never happened at a student reading, losing not one student but two. Yet Vinnie's situation is different. He's seventeen, and not a kid. He could legally go home on his own, although I wouldn't have allowed it. As for you, I saw you talking with your dad. Later, you said you were leaving with him. Ms. Carbone overheard our conversation. She'll be a witness in case there's a hearing."

I looked down at my dirty plate. "Do you think they'll fire you?"

He squeezed my hand. "No. The superintendent is a good guy. He's pleased that we'll be checking on Vinnie tonight. You don't mind going along?"

I shook my head. At the same time, I felt crappy, thinking I'd caused trouble for Mr. Ryan. Why hadn't I thought of him before I skipped out? As if reading my thoughts, he said, "Don't beat yourself up, Chris. Fourteen's an age when kids think about running away. They don't consider the consequences." He stood up. "Besides, all's well that ends well. Now let's go see Vinnie before I take you home."

Back on Route One, he said, "Do you feel like telling me about the spying?"

"I guess so." I waited a minute before launching into a short version of the episode with the Kirbys. "And now she must think I'm a real sicko," I said, "and she's right. Who else would do something so dopey?"

"You think you're the first guy to spy on a woman? What about Romeo, hanging outside Juliet's window?"

"They were like, the same age. This is different."

"We don't select the people we're attracted to. Sometimes it's an irresistible pull."

I thought of all the times I'd ridden my bike in the cold to Granite Cove Beach for a glimpse of Mrs. Kirby. I'd been powerless against the urge. "I guess that's how it was with me. I couldn't tell anyone about it because they'd think I was crazy."

"You felt guilty for watching her?"

"Yeah, I did."

"And when you got caught by the husband, you felt like a criminal, right?"

"Uh-huh."

"Have you ever heard the expression, 'You're only as sick as the secrets you keep?'"

"I have." I turned to him. "But I like secrets."

"I'm not saying they're bad. It's the secrets that make you feel guilty. Those aren't good."

Everett Hospital was an old-fashioned place with pea-soup-green walls and dim yellow lighting in the tiled corridors. The nurses wore stiff white caps from another era. After checking in at a reception desk, we took an ancient elevator to the third floor. No one noticed us as we roamed the halls searching for room three thirty-three. When we found it, we stood outside, peering in.

Vinnie was staring up at a TV on the wall. His upper chest was bandaged and his face bruised. He had a black eye. I followed Mr. Ryan into the room. Vinnie stared at us, looking from one to the other. "You guys look worse than me. Who jumped *you?*"

Mr. Ryan said, "Let's just say it's been a helluva night. How are you feeling, Vinnie?"

"You know what they say. 'It only hurts when I laugh.'"

Mr. Ryan rested his forearms on the metal railing running alongside the bed. "I feel responsible for what happened to you tonight. I'm sorry."

"Ah, it ain't your fault. I screwed outta the reading early. No one saw me leave."

I spoke up. "Vinnie will do anything to avoid sitting with Richie on the bus." He laughed, but immediately held up a hand. "Don't make me laugh. My ribs. It kills."

"We'll let you rest," Mr. Ryan said. "Is there anything we can do?"

"You can ask the school to send my homework. Doctor says I have to stay at least a week. A broken rib can puncture a lung, they tell me. It sucks, but at least my skull ain't broken."

"I'll personally see that the school sends your homework," Mr. Ryan said.

"I've been lying here thinking, 'cause I've got nothing else to do. I figure it's time I graduated from high school. There's life credits I can get to speed things up."

"That's a worthy goal," Mr. Ryan said.

Vinnie said, "I always wanted to join the Coast Guard, see the world. I'd like to be stationed in the South Pacific, like that artist guy. I'd retire to a little shack on the beach with a plot of land. In the morning, I'd gather driftwood and do wood carvings to sell to the tourists. My dad taught me to carve before he split. He said I was good."

"The artist you mentioned is Gauguin," Mr. Ryan said. "His paintings celebrate life on the islands. Maybe your wood carvings will do the same."

"First I've gotta graduate. If ya don't mind, how 'bout tossing in a couple books by those two Ray guys you mentioned?" Vinnie looked embarrassed. "Watching TV all day'll drive me nuts."

Mr. Ryan smiled. "Raymond Carver and Raymond Chandler. I'd be happy to."

We said goodbye and headed for the door. "Bye, Vinnie," I said, turning around.

"Thanks for comin'. And remember, don't party in East Boston."

"Don't worry," Mr. Ryan said. "We won't."

In the hospital parking lot, Mr. Ryan unlocked the car. "One last stop," he said, looking at me. "Home. How do you feel about that?"

"The truth? I feel lousy."

He backed out of the parking space. "There's an old Zen saying: 'The only way out is through.' I'm afraid that applies to your situation."

I looked out at the darkened street. "A big part of me wants to be on that bus, heading for New York City."

"Perfectly understandable."

Most of the houses on my street were in darkness when we arrived. Dad's car was in the driveway behind Mom's. I hoped Sherrie wasn't with him; things were bad enough. I clutched the door handle and turned to say goodbye to Mr. Ryan. "Thanks for what you did tonight—"

"I'm not letting you go in alone." He opened his door. "Tonight we're a team."

"Hey, thanks."

I scrambled out, following him up the driveway to the side door. Through a gap in the curtains, we saw Mom and Dad at the kitchen table staring into coffee mugs.

"Here goes," Mr. Ryan said, rapping on the glass pane.

Two seconds later Mom swung the door open. She made a lunge for me. Dad stood behind her, looking embarrassed. I struggled out of her arms and said, "Mom, Dad, this is my English teacher, Mr. Ryan."

Mom hugged him too. "You saved our son. How can we ever thank you?" She led him inside. "Would you like a glass of wine, Mr. Ryan, or a cocktail?"

Dad threw up his hands. "Ginger, why does it always have to be about drinking?"

She whipped around to face him. "I'm just being sociable, Roger—something you know nothing about."

Mr. Ryan held up a hand. "Please, let's sit down and talk for a moment. I don't want anything, thank you."

The three sat at the table while I hung out by the stove. Mr. Ryan looked over at me. "Chris, this concerns you as well. Please have a seat."

The only empty chair was between Mom and Dad. As soon as I sat, Mom leaned over and plonked a messy kiss on my cheek. I wrinkled my nose.

Now that Mr. Ryan had their attention, he began. "Mr. and Mrs. Koski, it seems that this family suffers from a lack of communication."

Dad piped up: "This conversation may be unnecessary, Mr. Ryan. Are you aware I've filed for custody of Christopher?"

"Let's focus on the main issue right now," Mr. Ryan said. "You two have a great son. I was proud of his reading tonight. His story was about a treasured childhood memory. It was that period when you were a family unit. For whatever reason—and I'm not judging you—you're not today. You've each gone your separate ways. But instead of working as a team, you've become alienated. What happened tonight illustrates the desperate measures a kid will take when he feels isolated. Running away, as Chris attempted, is a cry for help. Yet who's listening?"

We sat silently staring down at the table. I was too scared to look up. Dad was the first to speak. "Thank you, Mr. Ryan, for your honesty. I think we had to hear what you had to say. I'll make a better attempt to consider my son's needs."

"Our son, Roger," Mom added.

"Sorry, Ginger. That's what I meant—our son."

Mr. Ryan stood. "Time for me to go. I certainly won't have trouble sleeping tonight."

My parents rose, thanking him again. Mom hugged him one last time. This was accompanied by a flood of tears. Dad shook his hand. I walked Mr. Ryan to his car. Outside, the crickets were in full chorus. A big silver moon lit up the driveway.

He got into his beat-up Jetta and leaned out the window. "Remember what I said. Write it down, all the details about tonight, while it's fresh in your mind. Something tells me you'll be revisiting this in the years to come."

"And you'll play a big role, Mr. Ryan."

He gave me a thumbs-up and turned the ignition key. The car roared to life.

"Thanks for everything," I said. "See you Monday."

"See you, buddy." He turned on the headlights and drove away.

I watched him disappear down Neptune Avenue until he was swallowed up by the night. Standing in the shadows of a maple tree, I stared at the moon peeking out from behind the new leaves.

"Buddy," I whispered.

FIFTEEN

Early August was humid. Being outside was like having a damp flannel blanket over me. That's why I didn't mind working. Save 'n' Rave was always cool. The old people complained it was too cool, but they complained about everything. In the winter, they said the store wasn't warm enough.

During my break, I got a Dr. Pepper from the machine and took it outside. The humidity made the cold bottle slippery. I sat on a big sack of mulch and drank most of it. Just as I was thinking about going back inside, I spotted Dad's van pulling into the parking lot. I watched him get out of the car and approach the loading dock.

"Hi, Dad."

"Hi, son." He took off his cap and wiped his forehead. It was sunburned, along with his nose.

"Wanna sip?" I held up the bottle.

"No, thanks. I only have a minute. I wanted to ask if it's okay if we don't go to your grandparents' for dinner tonight."

I involuntarily smiled. Did I mind? It was the best news I'd heard all week. My grandparents, not surprisingly, have no air conditioning. Not only that, they won't open the windows. They keep the shades and curtains pulled against the sun, making the house as dark as a tomb. Grams says it stays cool that way. It doesn't. "No problem," I said. "What's up?"

After a quick glance around, he surprised me by lowering himself next to me on the mulch bag. I moved over to make room. "Well," he said, his voice low, "Sherrie and I are going into Boston to buy rings."

"Rings?"

He looked away. "You know ... wedding rings."

"You mean, like married people?"

He nodded. "I wanted you to hear it from me, Christopher. I'd like you to be my best man. We're getting married at the Lutheran church rectory on Wednesday, at five."

"You mean next Wednesday?" That was only a week away.

"It's just a simple ceremony. You see—you're old enough to know this—Sherrie's going to have a baby." He finally looked at me. Now his cheeks were as pink as his nose.

"A baby?" I felt like my brain had turned to cotton candy.

"Tests show it's a boy."

"You mean I'll finally have a brother?" I stared at him, my mouth open.

He smiled. "Looks that way." He rose to a standing position and gave me his hand, pulling me up. "I've got a lot to do in the meantime. I'm sorry about tonight, son."

"That's okay. Shawna Curran invited some kids to swim at her pool. I'll probably go there." I'd had to tell her I couldn't go because of a "prior commitment." She'd sounded disappointed.

"That's good. I'll be in touch with the details the next couple days." He placed a hand on my shoulder. "Thanks, son."

"Dad, can I tell Mom?"

He paused. "That's fine. She's invited to the wedding. Whether she goes or not is her decision."

After Dad left I stared into space, thinking about his news. While growing up, I'd constantly asked my parents for a brother; now it was finally happening. Of course, I hadn't imagined being fifteen when the kid arrived. That hadn't been in my plans. On the other hand, I could be the cool big brother who'd teach the kid cool stuff. I leaned against the wall, imagining the things we'd do together:

1.) I'd show him how to ride down the stairs in a cardboard box.

2.) I'd strap him to my back and take him on my skateboard.

3.) On Halloween we'd go trick-or-treating and fill his baby carriage with candy.

As always, Mr. Zagrobski interrupted my daydreaming. He shouted, "Koski, are you gonna stand there like a zombie? We got crates to unpack."

I went inside, still in a daze. Later I sat on my stool in Hygiene Supplies, stocking the shelves with soap, mouthwash, and false-teeth adhesive. When I looked up, Mrs. Kirby was coming down the aisle. Her legs, in white shorts, were tanned a bronze color. I got to my feet and greeted her. "If you need help with your order, I'll be happy to assist."

"Actually, Christopher, I may need help. My husband said to buy the biggest bag of charcoal in the store. Are they all on display?"

"Let me check." I scooted down the aisle and over to the grilling section. The twenty-pound bags were all gone. I went to the back of the store and found two bags propped against the wall. I returned to Mrs. Kirby. "We've got one out back. Want me to take your cart and put it inside?"

"Would you please? Thanks so much."

She pushed the cart toward me. I grabbed the handle bar, warm from her grip. After spinning the cart around, I raced off with a rattling and clanking. In the storage area, I tossed an oversize bag of charcoal into the cart. A couple of truck drivers standing in the doorway watched me. One whistled and called, "It's the Incredible Hulk!" I flexed my muscles and they laughed.

I returned to Mrs. Kirby. "Let me know when you check out. I'll put it in your car."

"I'm ready now," she said, "if that's okay with you."

I walked alongside her to the cash register and waited as she paid for her order. Together we walked through the parking lot. She glanced over at me. "Have you gotten taller? I remember when you reached my shoulder."

I blushed at the memory, yet I was pleased. I'd grown at least three inches since school got out. Now Mom asks me to reach stuff on the high kitchen shelves. "I suppose I have," I said with a shrug, like I hadn't noticed.

When we reached her car, I whisked the keys from her hand. "Allow me," I said, moving to the back. I placed the bag of groceries inside the station wagon. Taking a quick breath, I flexed and lifted the charcoal from the cart, putting it on its side. After that I closed the trunk and moved to the driver's side, unlocking the door. Finally, with a sweeping bow, I swung open the door, handing Mrs. Kirby the keys.

She laughed and slid onto the seat. Shielding her eyes from the sun, she looked up at me. "What in the world would I do without you, Christopher?"

"You wouldn't want to try, Mrs. Kirby." I shut the door and stood back.

She lowered her window. "Good," she said. "Then I won't."

I waited as she drove out of the lot. When she disappeared from view, I headed back inside the store.

The End

About the Author

Sharon Love Cook is the author of the Granite Cove Mysteries: *Come for the chowder, stay for the murder.* She and husband Oliver live in Beverly, Mass., a coastal town. They share their home with two ancient cats and one ancient dog.

If you enjoyed this book, the author would love an online review on Amazon.com. Thank you in advance.